I0764897

Frank Belknap Long circa 1932

WHEN CHAUGNAR WAK

WHEN CHAUGNAR WAKES

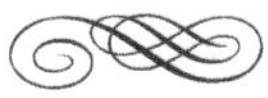

The Collected Poetry and Other Works of Frank Belknap Long

FRANK BELKNAP LONG

Edited by Perry M. Grayson

Tsathoggua Press

When Chaugnar Wakes:
The Collected Poetry and Other Works of Frank Belknap Long
Edited by Perry M. Grayson

Published by Tsathoggua Press
2/25 Redman Rd, Dee Why, NSW 2099, Australia
http://www.tsathogguapress.com

First Edition
ISBN: 978-1-7635245-0-7 (Hardcover)
ISBN: 978-1-7635245-1-4 (Ebook)
Cover designed by Perry M. Grayson
Tsathoggua Press colophon by Eric York

Contents

Introduction

Frank Belknap Long, Poet and Pauper

BY PERRY M. GRAYSON

Perhaps if Frank Belknap Long was born in France in the 1800s he might've actually been acknowledged by today's literati as a *Great Poet*. Gazing at a photo of the youthful Belknapius (as he was called by his best friend H. P. Lovecraft), one could easily imagine him as an elf-statured bard in the court of some ancient kingdom. I envision him puffing blue smoke out of a pipe—constructed from the bones of a creature straight out of Lord Dunsany's dreamworlds. But I have to pinch myself and wake up. Frank Long's verse and prose poetry was confined largely to amateur journals of the 1920s and early '30s, the pulp magazine *Weird Tales* and fantasy fanzines of the 1970s.

Your humble editor finds no fault with Lovecraft's observation that Long strove to remain lyrical when it came to style in his stories. In his critical essay "The Work of Frank Belknap Long, Jr.", Lovecraft wrote: "In November 1921, came 'In the Tomb of Semenses,' an Egyptian phantasy filled with musical and subtly rhythmical phrases, and opiate visions of 'multi-coloured lights and the clanging-to of brazen portcullises,' which proclaimed the genuine poet beneath a dress of prose." Even when writing a story meant to stick to a formula for a pulp magazine like *Thrilling Mystery* or a late 1960s gothic paperback, Long paid special attention to giving sections of prose a romantic and poetic quality. At his best, Long could weave prose with the same rhythm, color and imagery that his verse did, as in this excerpt from the story "The Timeless Man" (1945):

> *The transparency wavered and changed shape, becoming conical and then spherical. Like a great, rainbow-hued water bubble it settled to rest directly in front of the canvas, its base flattening as the aliens continued to knead it with their minds.*
>
> *Deep-cradled were the first faint stirrings of life; fluted and fragile, like a sighing cocoon caught in a gust of luminous wind. A twisting and swaying and a hungry reaching out for a nourishing flame that was both breath and substance.*
>
> *Breath and more life… and ever more life… until there came into view in the depths of the web the outlines of a human shape.*

Notice FBL's particular attention to consonance ("faint stirrings of life; fluted and fragile")—a technique Poe was very fond of.

Long's worldview pertaining to art is also summed up in "The Timeless Man," when a character says 'Life is short but art is long, or, if you prefer eternal. It may be a thumping platitude, but I happen to believe it.' It's surely Long's own voice, speaking through this character, commenting on why people create art: 'It was the man's glory—the one thing that set him apart from the brutes.' Surely a bit of romanticism there, but if you're looking for something more lyrical and focusing on *love* itself, we need look no further than FBL's science fiction tale "The Flame of Life" (1939):

> *Marshall said: "I am godlike now! A man in love is very close to the eternal."*
>
> *But Marshall did not hear him. He saw again moonlight haloing red-gold hair, dappling a white throat. He saw her face again, luminous with tenderness. He saw her standing*

in a dim-lit vestibule, waving at him. He heard her whisper: "Tomorrow, Thomas, Tomorrow!"

Happiness enveloped him like a flame, swirling up about him in a golden blaze.

It would seem that there are some who think poetry is as dead as the gods in Long's verse "Sonnet." Nevertheless, some evidence of how FBL's poems appeal to a modern man comes in this comment from Marshall B. Tym in *Horror Literature: A Core Collection and Reference Guide* (1988): "Long's poems have active verbs and *move*, and they are clear and musical."

Dreams are a thing for the young, or the young at heart, but Frank Belknap Long managed to hold onto a bit of that youthful sense of wonder until his later years. His output may have decreased considerably during his last two decades, but he actually returned to craft a few more poems. In *Autobiographical Memoir* (Necronomicon Press, 1985), the geriatric Long addressed the topic of the youthful daydreamer: "...there are worlds of strangeness and wonder which can never be reentered in adult years, or that the memories of adults can never hope to recapture in more than a transitory, infinitely incomplete way. It is in those worlds that the wisdom of children seems often to transcend every sophisticated insight acquired by adults through their vastly greater experience and orientation to what is commonly thought of as reality in the course of the years."

Most people shed their dream-quests—if they have any at all—shortly after their teens. But Long remained a castaway in two dimensions for the majority of his life. One half eked out a miserable existence in the "real world," while the other journeyed to realms and ages afar. Long may have been—financially at least—a pauper for most of his life, but as a poet he attained glittering gems more valuable than the treasure troves of a Spanish galleon. And as you'll read here, the gifted bard was alive and well even while FBL was a young man of 20.

A Note on the Texts

BY PERRY M. GRAYSON

This volume collects all the known poetry in existence by Frank Belknap Long. It includes fragments and full poems found in letters and stories. In addition, this volume renders my first two out of print 1995 Tsathoggua Press chapbooks (*The Eye Above the Mantel and Other Stories* and *The Darkling Tide: Previously Uncollected Poetry*) obsolete. "Nostalgia," a Long poem mentioned in a July 7, 1923 letter from Clark Ashton Smith to FBL, is to my knowledge no longer extent. I and several colleagues have searched high and low for it to no avail.

The long wait has ended for those who have sought after *The Eye Above the Mantel* specifically. The present collection likewise hopes to correct the few typos the crept into those early Tsathoggua Press chapbooks.

Much to my delight in the years following the publication of *The Darkling Tide*, "Unhappiness," the one fugitive prose poem mentioned in my note on that text was located by stalwart Lovecraftian scholar S. T. Joshi. Other previously undiscovered poems were discovered by your humble editor and Kenneth W. Faig in exhaustive searches through various amateur journals of the 1920s and 1930s. In particular, Faig unearthed the prose poem vignette "Sandaris" in Lovecraft correspondent C. W. Smith's *The Tryout*. It is entirely possible that still more obscure Long pieces remain buried in those ephemeral small publications. Sources of previously uncollected items and those that appeared in *The Darkling Tide* are cited. Should "Nostalgia" or any additional items be located, a future revised edition of *When Chaugnar Wakes* will include them.

Recent years have seen the publication of the complete poetical works of Long's best friend and mentor Lovecraft as well as their peer, Clark Ashton Smith. *When Chaugnar Wakes* now joins their ranks after 25 years in the making. It's hoped that this tome will further contribute to the appreciation of the work of those literary men who sought to preserve the tradition of fantastic and romantic poetry in the 20th century.

The quest to publish this book spanned two continents and began when I was only 19 years-old. It was a task that required plenty of in-depth research. It sent me across the U.S. from my Southern California home to the east coast and put me in touch with many experts in the weird fiction field. It followed me on my relocation Down Under. I've made quite a few friends along the way, without whose assistance this book would be drastically incomplete.

For their help and/or general encouragement, support and enthusiasm I would like to thank: my wife Tanya, Rob Preston, Donald Sidney-Fryer, Rah Hoffman (R.I.P), S. T. Joshi, David E. Schultz, Scott Briggs, Bob Price, Derrick Hussey, Steve T. Miller, Marc Michaud, Ben Indick (R.I.P.), Peter H. Cannon, Stefan Dziemianowicz, Ken Faig, Bob Knox, Sam Moskowitz (R.I.P.), Ron Hilger, Dennis Rickard, Joe Wrzos (R.I.P), Dwayne Olson, Phil Rahman (R.I.P.), Keith Allen Daniels (R.I.P.), Alan Gullette, Richard Bleiler, Don Burleson, Danny Lovecraft, Leigh Blackmore, Brad Verter, Will Murray, Eric York, T.E.D. Klein and Mark Berman.

Preface to A MAN FROM GENOA by Samuel Loveman

Homer was the first and greatest of romantic poets. Helen with her filleted golden hair and cupped breasts, on whom the shadow of no elder civilization has ever fallen, has her moments of deific depth, but it is a depth evolved from the supremely romantic mind, not the outwelling of supremely tragic poetry. Strife there may be in all of this, but tragedy is to follow later if it is to follow at all. In the meantime one may well be content with the ancient, beautiful things—gold, raiment and gems, perfumes ascending sheer from braziers into a blue world, with men and women glamorously conceived as a foil for the unworthiness of actual life.

Frank Belknap Long, then, is our new poet. At twenty-three we find him writing poems for his first, glorious volume—poems that might have been penned by the greatest of the lesser Elizabethans, with at least one, "The Marriage of Sir John de Mandeville," worthy of Christopher Marlowe.

To Long the hideousness of life as it may be found in the modern city ceases to exist, but in his refusal of realism as his contemporaries see it there lies a shining road to finer things, and to the momentum of pity that spins into permanence all tragic and major poetry.

A Knight of La Mancha

"The stars," he said, "are very low,
The sky above them arches so,
And hieroglyphics of the night
Have robbed the moon of touch and sight:
But Sancho, did the lanterns glow
Above La Mancha long ago?

"Why, Sancho, in the narrow streets
Ragged boys sold kites and sweets;
And like San Pedro's cross there flamed
A dozen inns where unashamed
We munched on cheese and fancy meats,
And you were tossed in yellow sheets.

"And then we woke with sudden fear
And saw the mountains disappear
Beyond the road, above the town;
For mountains move, and tumble down!
Sancho, Sancho, do you hear?
Mountains *walk*—with no one near!"

Miguel de Cervantes, author of DON QUIXOTE (1547 - 1616)

The Marriage of Sir John de Mandeville

Because the King of Travelers
Had sworn that he would wive
The golden roofs were thronged with heads
Of every lad alive.

A thousand shawms were lightly blown,
A thousand drums were beat;
And young Sir John de Mandeville
Came riding down the street.

He was a wiry knight and brave,
A foolish knight, and wise;
And he had flaming caravans
And suns within his eyes.

"The Troglodytes," he spoke with heat,
"Have bells upon their toes;
They sleep in caves on yellow leaves
And flap their ears at foes."

Sir John, he paused, and wet his lips,
The people crowded nearer;
His words were honey-dew and wine

To every famished hearer.

"In Asia in the gray-white lands
Beyond the fields of Gog
There dwell a million unicorns
That caper in the fog.

"And there are men whose swollen lips
Do overlap their faces;
Men of girth and men of thin
And darkish pygmy races!"

"The sea of gravel ebbs and flows
As other seas do not:
Upon its banks of brackish sand
The golden fishes rot.

"I've been to lands of fibrous fruits
Where men are born full-grown;
Great bearded tots who cry and laugh
And suck their thumbs and moan.

"They're fed on milk and griffin's eggs
Until they reach their prime;
And that's at eighty odd or more—
And then they lisp in rhyme.

"And I have wooed the Amazons
Who hate all sickly men;
They kill their infants if they show
A weakness in their ken.

"And I have been to Egypt-land
And seen the nodding Sphinx

Who sleeps a thousand years and then
Awakes and slyly winks.

"And I have seen a head that had
No body for its mate:
It lay upon a grassy slope
And ate and ate and ate.

"And I have talked with Prester John,
With Kubla Khan, and kings
Of hollow lands, whose eyes are green,
Who love all loveless things.

"And I have watched the cranes uprise
Against a sky of gold,
Beyond the Land of Darkness
Where night is, and the cold.

"And no manner of man may fare
Unto the frozen world;
For there all ends and he would be
Into the heavens hurled.

"And there are lands upon which mists
Have settled like a shroud;
And lands where Silence is the Law
And none may speak aloud.

"And I have watched the satyrs dance
By lonely inland meres;
And I have held a brimming bowl
To catch a dragon's tears.

"And I have seen the cockatrice,

The kraken and the roc;
The hippogriff, and tityus
And blue-eyed Scythian cock.

"And I have seen the Isle of Spice,
The Isle of Silver Laughter;
The Moving Isle, the Isle of Fruits
And the Dark Isle after."

But then young Mandeville he turned
And saw his gracious bride;
Her eyes were gleaming as she rode,
Her hair was blowing wide.

And Sir Knight laughed a merry laugh,
And swore that he would be
No more a weary traveler
Beyond the China Sea.

They entered in the church at dawn,
The kneeling bishops sang;
And Mandeville was wed, and then
The silver bells they rang.

Because a weary traveler
Had sworn that he would wive
The golden roofs were thronged with heads
Of every lad alive.

Woodcut of Sir John De Mandeville

A Man from Genoa

I saw a man from Genoa
Who turned and smiled at me,
And something in his wistful gaze
Was like a blasted tree.

He told me then that he had come
With flaming plumes and vair,
And cloths of saffron and of gold,
And vests of camel's hair.

And he had beads from Carthage
And silks from windy Tyres,
And tiny chests of spikenard
Preserved from Illium's fires.

And once in gracious Babylon.
Where virtue is unknown,
He bought a girl from distant Ind
With bits of colored stone.

The man who came from Genoa
Had sorrow in his eyes,
And yet he turned and smiled at me
And made a stout surmise.

"My silks, they say, are waterlogged,
My spears and helmets worn;
And yet I came from Genoa
Around the southern horn.

"The Lords of War have laughed at me
And will not take my vests!
They are too small and fiberless
To span their thunderous chests."

And then I somehow pitied him
And bought the worthless things,
The silks and grails and parakeets
And gold and copper rings.

I have them yet and know quite well
They're uselessness to me;
And yet the man from Genoa—
His eyes were like the sea!

I saw him go upon the quay
And whistle through his hands;
I saw his galley swing to port
Above the yellow sands.

The ship that veered before the wind
Had green and scarlet sails;
And turbaned prophets paced the poop
And Nubians thronged the rails.

He waved his hand, and jumped aboard
And danced upon the deck;
And then I saw him take command
And clear the harbor wreck.

They passed a town with marble streets
And spires of malachite;
Where centaurs worshipped headless gods
Whose limbs were zoned with light.

I saw them sail into the East—
And now in far Cathay
I seek the man from Genoa
Who bore my gold away.

Manhattan Skyline

The West is bright with stones that rise,
Ships go down to the sea with flags:
Did Marlowe dream such topless towers
Shivering in his tavern rags?

Come, Let Us Make

Come, let us make a peacock tune
And stroll about the garden,
And take our magic from the moon
And never beg its pardon.

There are so very many things
We do not know at all:
Did Rachel wear her hair in rings?
Was Heliogabalus tall?

Had David fifty hundred sheep?
Was Simon Magus right?
Was Sheba's Queen a negress?
Are Virgil's stanzas trite?

A man may go on living
And never ask
If Shelley wore pajamas,
If Dante wore a mask.

But we'll get answers from the moon
And never beg its pardon
And when we know we'll make a song
And stroll about the garden.

The Magi

"A King shall be born to the Jews,
A King to the Jews," they said;
They chafed their hands to keep them warm,
And they shared their bitter bread.

They lay in their folds of sheepskin
Under the starry sky;
And like the warrior gods of Rome
The silver clouds went by.

"A Child shall be born to glory!
A Child in the winter night:
He shall reign in grace and beauty
His head shall be crowned with light!

"A Child shall be born to glory!"
The white stars beckoned and sang:
"He shall reign in grace and beauty!"
The bells of the shepherds rang.

But one arose and prophesied
Whose face was wet with tears:
"No King shall reign in Israel
For twenty thousand years!"

"A King shall be born to the Jews,

A King to the Jews," they said.
"But He shall wear a crown of thorns,
Of thorns upon his head."

They lay in their folds of sheepskin
Under the starry sky;
And like the warrior gods of Rome
The silver clouds went by.

Walt Whitman

They've based a creed upon his life
That was so rich and merry;
But I prefer to think of him
In glory on a ferry.

Poet Walt Whitman (1819 - 1892)

An Old Tale Retold

"We sail tomorrow on the tide,"
Sir Richard Grenville said:
"Lord Howard thinks the ships of Spain
Will turn his kerseys red!"

All night Sir Richard lay and groaned
And swore that this would be
The last of Howard's twenty ships
To weigh and stand to sea.

And when the Spanish moon went out
And my Lord flagged: "Retreat!"
Sir Richard spat upon the deck
And cursed upon his feet.

"Does my Lord Howard think that we
Are made of Spanish clay?
Has my Lord Howard never seen
An Englishman at bay?

"A man were better gray and dead
And buried fathoms deep.
We serve the Queen, by grace of God!
And does he think we're sheep?"

Sir Richard leaned upon the rail
And whistled through his hands,
"I'm master of this ship," he said,
"And give my own commands!"

The Spanish ships were fifty-two
And Grenville's ship was small;
But yet he smiled, and down its length
There ran the boatswain's call.

The galleons of Spain were tall
And Grenville's ship rode low;
But yet he smiled down its length
White forms ran to and fro.

The Spanish ships came slowly on
And Grenville stood at bay;
And when they opened fire his hat;
And wig were shot away.

For twenty hours Sir Richard stood
And gave them shot for shot;
He stood upon his feet and fought
Until his teeth were hot.

His men came crawling on their knees
To curse the satin Don;
And some came crawling though they had
No knees to crawl upon.

Five thousand Spaniards strove to put
Sir Richard in the sea;
But still he stood and fought and fought
With tigers on his lee.

But fifty ships are fifty ships
And even Britons tire.
And when a man's consumed with hate
He often misses fire.

And so they took him in his shoes
Before the night was spent;
But every Spaniard doffed his hat
And cheered him when he went.

Prediction

I do not think that I shall see
The moon, nor any linden tree,
Nor flaming orchards in the dawn
But that I'll know they're made for me.

And I shall hold my goblet up
And drink the dizzy wine of kings,
And seek cool cheeks, and tingling song
And all the gorgeous, golden things.

The Prophet

He stood by the river and whistled through his hands
And ibises from Egypt filled the morning lands;
They circled in the air, and their wings caught the sun
And they turned gold and crimson 'ere his song was done.

I knew he was a prophet, and I swore by my hat
To place on Hathor's altar a yellow tiger-cat;
But then he somehow heard me, and though I tried to fly
He turned and cursed, and I became—a shadow on the sky!

A Time Will Come

A time will come when we shall share
The wonder, dear, together,
Of flaming candles on a shrine
In gray and golden weather.

And we shall kneel with avid eyes
To watch a shining chalice
By children borne across the nave
Of some cathedral-palace.

And we shall rise, and go away
With eager lips that cling,
Unmindful of the strumming choirs
And every living thing.

When We Have Seen

When we have seen Spring's blossoms
And the apple itself decay,
Is there any need for fasting?
Shall we loiter another day?

Let us mount gorgeous horses
Caparisoned for the moon;
For sea-girt cities beckon
And we go Troyward soon.

The cup of the moon is hollow,
We hold it now in our hands,
The golden flasks are flowing
Throughout the morning lands.

Then let us go with gladness
And making of happiest song,
While the sheepsmen on the mountains
Hurry the flocks along.

When we have seen Spring's blossoms
And the apple itself decay,
Is there any need for fasting?
Shall we loiter another day?

In Antique Mood

I am afraid, for every slender dream
Has burst its sheath, and were I now to blow
The ancient pipe the ancient god would seem
A form gigantic, and I fear him so.
His hoof-beats are too rhythmic, are too loud;
They clatter in my brain, and when at night
I draw the sheets, I seem to draw my shroud:
The goat would trample me if I should fight.

But you a steadfast, jealous watch will keep.
You tender me your lips and fallen hair
As safeguard: there is solace when I sleep
Beside you, O compassionately fair!
But even on your arms there falls a shade—
Dear, hold me close! I am afraid... afraid.

A Sonnet for Seamen

I do not think that men who praise the sea,
Who praise tall ships, and wrecks and goodly sails,
Who tar their hair, and laugh at northern gales
Have reckoned with the sea's perversity;
For it will take the silent heart and soul
With floods of loneliness and wild desire
To sail in some old galley out of Tyre
On jasper gulfs beyond a ragged shoal.

I do not think that men who love the waves,
Who talk of boats and fogs and creaking spars,
Have thought of how long seas and flaming stars
Can send poor lads awhirling to their graves:
Men praise the sea's tyrannic majesty—
But that's what eats the heart and soul of me!

In Hospital

The rapid steps of an approaching nurse
Beat on my ears; I hear again the groans
Of patients in Ward 2, uncivil moans
Of wretches taking ether with a curse;
I gaze upon the ceiling, bear the smell
Of chloroform with half-assumed chagrin:
Then someone says, "My god, but you are thin!"
And, "Aren't you ever going to get well?"

Then bandages are torn from tired chests,
And arms are punctured where they're sore and blue;
But I am off on legendary quests
Of glamor with a mad, quixotic crew.
I lie and dream of Casanova's folly,
I tramp the English downs with Mr. Polly.

Florence

It was not gold which made thy name so great,
For richer cities have not fared as thou;
It was the crown of strife upon thy brow
Which genius hammered in the teeth of fate:
For the great sons did praise thee when they died,
Like flames they soared in sorrow and despair;
They loved thee as a woman loves her hair,
They loved thee as a lover loves his bride.

The Exile shared with thee his bitter bread,
And Leonardo his inventiveness;
Savonarola loved thy holy dead,
The Medici thy wars and scarlet dress;
Not even Venice when she wed the sea
Was bound as were thy mighty sons to thee.

On Reading Arthur Machen

There is a glory in the autumn wood,
The ancient lanes of England wind and climb
Past wizard oaks and gorse and tangled thyme
To where a fort of mighty empire stood:
There is a glamor in the autumn sky;
The reddened clouds are writhing in the glow
Of some great fire, and there are glints below
Of tiny yellow where the embers die.

I wait, for he will show me, clear and old,
High-raised in splendor, sharp against the North
The Roman eagles, and through mists of gold
The marching legions as they issue forth:
I wait, for I would share with him again
The ancient wisdom, and the ancient pain.

Arthur Machen (1863 - 1947)

Two Stanzas for Master François Villon

A man there was who had no hair at all
To warm a graceless and a chastened head:
For thirty winters had he known the fall
Of leaves upon the stones his feet would tread
Until his hopes, and all his fears were dead.

A man there was who had no teeth nor hair,
And Justice stalked him till he nimbly fled;
But though his cronies walked upon the air,
And though the devil mapped the life he led,
He somehow glittered—and his songs are read!

François Villon

The Rebel

He walked in caverns, talked with eager men
Whose thoughts were bent on barter, gain and loss:
He saw the worlds which center in the toss
Of one small coin; and he was wretched then.
He hated cities and their iron marts;
He longed for palms against a sunset sky;
His only friends were lads with sea-tamed hearts;
He loved tall masts and great ships scudding by.

For there are men who never sail in ships,
Who cannot bide the thought of any land;
As children they awake with muted lips,
Amazed by endless leagues of sunlit sand;
As children they awake, and seeking, find
The black monsoon and gulls upon the wind.

In the Garden of Eros (Theocritus)

I'll mark the spot where Eros comes to woo,
For nature follows happy fancies there;
On gorgeous mounds rich-grown with maidenhair,
In gardens where the crisping myrtles blew,
She whispers to the winds as thrushes do,
Her wealthy fruitage she can scarcely bear
While love is telling all the world she's fair,
And adds for spite a million kisses, too.

And you might dream of matted honey-vines,
And you would find the sky forever blue,
Or be a happy bird and lisp the lines
Which sea-green Galatea made you rue,
Or sip a million sips of laughing wines
With just your love upon the grass with you.

Cover of *The Goblin Tower* (1949 chapbook edition)

In Mayan Splendor

In misty dreams and shadowed memories
Of fabled cities I have dwelt apace;
And from strange springs set round with guardian trees
Have slaked my thirst, and scornful of the face
Of harsh reality have stooped to trace
Dark figures on the sands of alien keys:
In Mayan splendor I have spanned the seas
And clothed myself in legendary grace.

In Copan I have dwelt where serpent stones
And skies of dusky violet merge to form
A glimmering gate of wonder whereto bones
Of warrior dead are gathered in a storm
Of whirling clouds and crimson flames that roar
Beneath the sky-vault where great condors soar.

The White People

Out of the grass when the dew is wet
Their houses lean and their hoards are set
Deep in the woods that are not yet.

Out of the earth when the night is cold
Their worm-dogs leap and over the wold
They fly with tales that are not told.

Out of the wold when the moon rides low
Their witch-fires flicker and tapers glow
To guide the goblins to and fro.

Out of the lake when the comets pass
Their maidens rise; and over the grass
They crawl like shadows on a glass.

Out of the East when the stars spin high
They dance and dance and the years go by
And the sun and moon fade out of the sky—

And still they dance.

An Old Wife Speaketh It

Once witches danced upon this green
And held unhallowed revel,
And rings of somber grass were seen
Attesting of the Devil.

Once little people gamboled here
With symbols writ in white,
Whose faces bore an impious fear
Beneath a red moon's light.

Here lingered once the godless dead
In legions never numbered,
With painted eyeballs in each head;
While Blessed Saints have slumbered.

A corpse once laid can rise again
As has been twice attested:
But oh, the misery and pain
Of dead souls so molested!

A centuried sin can body take
And pierce man with its look,
And plenilunal magic make,
As writ in Holy Book.

And ah, the shameless funeral feast

Within the drunken bower,
When mindless matter apes the beast
With maleficious power.

The serpent's sting, the smell of goat,
The blue and scarlet fires,
The succubi who foully gloat
Upon their lewd desires!

Once witches danced upon this green
And held unhallowed revel,
And rings of somber grass were seen
Attesting of the Devil.

Stallions of the Moon

Under granite ledges,
Over phantom sands,
Race the milk-white horses
From the Umber Lands.

Under granite ledges—
Hooves of golden sheen
Flashing in the twilight,
Purple cliffs between.

Mystic beasts of Sibyl,
Fed on golden oats,
More than Spartan finish
On their moonspun coats.

Argent waters check them:
Now they take the air,
Snorting hippogriffins
Speeding starward there.

See them in the gloaming,
Bridges flying free!
Underneath the red stars,
Mounts for you and me!

Advice

Down the stairs and up the street
The kobolds go on silent feet;
And two by two the Fears parade
From portico to balustrade;
And stealing from a hidden place
The tiny goblins grin and race:
Carouse, my friend, with such as these,
And shun the bloated things that wheeze!

The Goblin Tower

The Goblin Tower stood and stood
And stood for years and years:
And it was haunted splendidly
By twenty thousand Fears.

The Gears were tall and very old,
With scars upon their faces;
And there were Greek and Hindoo Fears,
And Fears of Saxon races.

The Tower's windows looked upon
A moat of thunderous green;
And red lights shone behind the panes
Where gallant ghosts had been.

The ghosts were shyer than the rats
That lived in Roland's hall;
And they reposed upon the chairs
Or walked upon the wall.

Until the Fears took up the lance
And chased them screaming hence;
And now they wander in the moat
Or climb the castle fence.

I dreamed the Goblin Castle fell

And vanished in the night:
And yet for years and years and years
It was a gorgeous sight.

The Inland Sea

I know a sea within a western land,
Where winds of silence blow, and all forlorn
The black waves wash, from lonely morn to morn,
Upon a gale-blown stretch of whitened sand.
No petrels sweep above that somber strand,
No living thing of any creature born,
Save on the hilltops where a sullen band
Of gaunt wolves crouch beneath the lunar horn.

In icy shallows polar lilies grow,
Which sunder to reveal Jurassic clay;
A bullet-head with motions weird and slow
Precedes a bulk which drives the wolves away:
A dark and monstrous lizard shape that glides
Upon the waters with the inland tides.

On Icy Kinarth

I dreamed I stood upon a buttressed ledge
Of Icy Kinarth. High above my head
Soared lizard-birds, and bats with wings outspread,
And loathsome tails that swept the mountain's edge,
A thousand rods below me streamed the sea,
Its black waves lapping at the Isles of Spice:
I clung in terror to a blasted tree,
And fought for footing on the slippery ice.

There came at last, by scent or instinct led,
A fleshless thing with glazed, malignant eyes:
It pawed my mouth until its claws were red,
And voiced its ire in sharp, metallic cries:
A dry and corpsy gargoyle-shape that fed
Its belly with the refuse of the skies.

Great Ashtoreth

The priests decreed that Ashtoreth should die,
And to the hills they bore her gilded throne;
And then for bread they gave to her a stone,
And pointed to the rock where she must lie.

Then quickly to the town they sped in glee,
And shut the gates, and to the people said:
"Great Ashtoreth the Sorceress is dead,
Great Ashtoreth is dead eternally."

But one by one the young men stole away,
And sought the hills and never more were seen:
And one by one the priests grew old and lean,
And there was wailing in the streets alway.

When Chaugnar Wakes

A billion miles beyond the suns
Which gild the edge of space,
Great Chaugnar dreams, and there is hate
And fury on its face.

Beyond the universe of stars
Where red moons wane and swim,
Great Chaugnar stirs, and heaves its bulk
Upon a crater's rim.

Its ropy arms descend to suck
Dark nurture from the deeps
Of lava-pools within a cone
That shines whilst Chaugnar sleeps.

Explorers of the outer stars
Have glimpsed that glowing cone;
Have glimpsed the vast and silent shape
Asleep upon its throne.

Explorers from the world we know
Have seen that shape in dreams;
Have watched its shadow fall and spread
On dim, familiar streams.

When Chaugnar wakes, its mindless hate

Will send it voyaging far;
It may set Sirius adrift,
Or seek a humbler star.

A humbler star with satellites,
Small planets in its train:
And that is why I kneel and kneel
Before Great Chaugnar's fane.

Chaugnar Faugn, inspired by FBL's "When Chaugnar Wakes" and "The Horror from the Hills"
by Robert H. Knox

Night-Trees

I thought I saw them writhing in the dawn
On cold, black hills—the gnarled and twisted ghosts
Of Titan cedars and the sapling hosts
That stood so starkly naked and forlorn.
Poor stricken things that bore the forms of men
And forms of beasts; great gorgons unreclaimed
By childhood's gracious fancy. Did I then
Declare that they had been forever maimed?

Tall aspens writhing like beheaded snakes,
And cypresses with lean, distorted necks,
And stunted hemlocks in the riven brakes
That fringed the garments of the oaken wrecks.
Oh, did I stand and curse them, one by one,
That were so lovely once beneath the sun?

The Horror on Dagoth Wold

"I have it here," he said, and stroked the rust
Upon his box—his eyes were twin dark stars—
"Medusa's head that turns desire to dust!
They buried it a fathom deep on Mars.

"I waited till the stars were right, and then
I robed myself in ermine flaked with gold.
And with a silver spade, unwatched by men,
I crept to where it lay in Dagoth Wold.

"I crept to where it lay, and working fast,
I drew it from its red and sentient tomb;
From jellied earth that whispered in the gloom,
And mired my feet until I woke at last."
"You woke?" I stared at him in pained surprise,
Forgetful of the star-glint in his eyes.

"To futile toil," he said, "our race is bound,
And to the waking world it must return:
Some vileness in us makes us scorn and wound
The shapes of flame for which our spirits yearn.

"But men go back again to dreams for things
They left behind; perchance to fetch a cloak,
Or gather up a batch of stolen rings,
Or catch a word some sweet, soft woman spoke.

"I have it here," he said, and tapped the lid
Upon his box—his eyes were twin dark stars—
"When Perseus died they sought to keep it hid,
And buried it a fathom deep on Mars."

The Abominable Snow Men

Blue shadows lay upon the crater's rim,
And far above the town a traveler moved
In circles through the snow; his eyes were dim
From glint of sun on ice in worlds unproved

A thousand feet below him at an inn
His host smiled wanly, said: "The fool will find
Small prints upon the snow-so small, so thin—
He will not know that they are prints which bind."

"He will not know that they are prints which bind!"
His very words gained substance on a height,
As to his knees the traveler fell, half-blind,
And groveled in the dimness of his sight.

"They dwell in barrows on a skyward wold
And make no sound; shrill hunger is their goad:
'Tis said they feed on men when men are bold;
When men are scarce, on flesh of fowl or toad."

The silence on the heights gave way to shrieks
As to a shattered cairn the traveler clung
And fought a shape with bright and slimy streaks
Of blood upon its fat, protruding tongue.

They came in swarms from out the crater's rim;
The thin snow men, abominable and cold;
They came in swarms, and tore him limb from limb,
And strewed his flesh in ribbons on the wold.

Exotic Quest

With windblown hair, and somber eyes alight,
Death kneels upon the moonlit silver sands,
A coral viper 'twixt her soft white hands,
While pale flamingoes pass in solemn flight.

To seek her there I came in morning years
With ghostly galleons, past sunless miles
Of lonely vineyards on Cyrenian Isles
Where golden griffins bathe in midnight meres.

Upon the far, white meadows of the sea,
Through some dim crest of mystic ocean foam,
My tired black bones in silent anguish roam—
For Death with weary arms enfolded me.

Pirate-Men

When pirate-men come in from sea
Their beards are stiff and black;
They sit them down and drink red ale,
With honey-wine and sack.

I know that pirates can endure
The laughter of the wise,
For they have nights of revelry,
And suns within their eyes.

And pirate-men remember more
Of what is wine to me
Than some who sit and talk and talk
And talk about the sea!

The charm and lure of pirate-men
Is something strange and clean,
Like leagues and leagues of yellow sand,
Or palms that dip and lean.

When pirate-men come in from sea
Their beards are stiff and black;
They sit them down and drink red ale,
With honey-wine and sack.

Subway

I sit between a Jewess whose tired eyes
Are glued on Dostoevsky, and a youth
With frittered mackintosh who reads: "When Ruth
Came in from third—" My interest quickly dies:
But then a stranger tramps upon my feet
And lights go out. "Quit shoving! Can't you see
That if you push you'll never get a seat?"

But here are sailors from the seven seas,
And laughing merchants from a street of walls,
And girls who dance all night in flaming halls;
And here are ruin, splendor and disease.
I thought: "How all this glitter, mirth and play
Would please Petronius or Rabelais!"

Sonnet

The gods are dead. The earth has covered them,
And they are less than shadows in our sight;
Young Helios is banished from delight,
Who once wore flame upon his garment's hem.
The world was young when tall Osiris died,
And it was old when Bacchus ceased to be;
A Light there was that towered deathlessly,
But once again has He been crucified.

The world is lonely now without its gods;
We stand forlorn beneath the stars of heaven,
For unto us no new joy can be given,
And we must always bear the bitter rods
Of heat and frost and harsh necessity:
There are no wonders now on land or sea.

The Hashish Eater

The boat was waiting; seas like foaming wine
Curled round its prow; the moon was full and red.
"I go," he laughed, "to lie upon her bed
And kiss her mouth until desire is dead,
For I am Caesar, and the world is mine!"
He shrieked, and woke upon a cross; his bands
Were dripping blood upon the yellow sands,
And far below a harlot wrung her hands.

Ballad of Mary Magdalene

The sun and moon and stars, she found,
Were hateful in her sight;
She cursed the stones, and cursed the bread,
And cursed the bitter night.

“I saw,” she said, “a sunless court
Where age had jostled youth,
And one who laughed when he was asked:
‘But tell me – where is truth?’”

“They slew a lad upon a hill
Who shared our sinner’s wine;
And there was not a braver lad
In all of Palestine.

“I stood and watched him when he hung
Upon the gallows tree,
And this I know: that he had eyes
For me – and only me.

“In Nazareth the violets creep
Between the jutting stones
Of desert-rim, and sepulcher,
And Israelitish bones.

“I hate all priests and Sadducees,

They're more than I can bear;
I'll go to Corinth and to Rome,
And sell my body there!"

Ballad of Saint Anthony

When Anthony was seventeen
And leaner than a tree,
By day and night he scourged his flesh
That hated chastity.

When Anthony was seventeen
He fasted night and day;
He scarcely tasted wine and meat,
And eggs he sent away

When Anthony was seventeen
He thought: "I fear the bark,
The talons of the dog, God keep
My soul when it is dark."

But Anthony was very young,
And youth must sleep and dream,
And what is murdered in the day
Will wake at night and scream.

So listen to the tale I tell,
And do not mourn or grieve,
For virtue lost at seventeen
Is not beyond retrieve.

When Anthony had prayed and prayed

Until his lips were white,
He drew of breeches, blouse and shoes,
And blew upon the light.

And then in darkness he lay down
Upon his narrow cot,
And what was murdered in the day
Came back and left him not.

And as he tossed from side to side
Upon his wretched bed,
The Holy Saints grew pale with shame
And midnight hung its head.

For she had bells upon her toes
And fillets on her brow,
But every inch of space between
Was white as virgin snow.

And every inch of space between
Set Anthony afire:
Alas, that such a goodly youth
Should burn with such desire!

Alas, that such a goodly youth
Should think, "I can't escape!
O must I then be slaughtered by
This beast in woman's shape?"

Yet lo! he flung her arms aside
And rolled upon the floor,
And screaming, ran with naked feet
To beat upon the door.

"O let me out!" he shrieked and prayed,
"For there are succubi

Upon my heels, and I am lost!
O heaven pity me!"

But as he screamed and sought to wake
The Holy Brotherhood,
She bent and kissed his lips and eyes,
And he—was turned to wood.

Yet it was something less than death
That to his lot befell,
And it was sweeter in his sight
Than marigolds in hell.

My tale is done; but men who sit
In judgment on our sins
Will never know the joy he got,
Because they sleep on pins.

West Indies

Black Guinea's blood, in agony congealed
By sweat and faggot, soothes the scented dust
And velvet rose on petaled rose of Spain:
Beside the sea, where shards of cannon rust,
The thing that once was done is done again;
The shape is formed that fecundates the sealed
And darkened womb of earth's enormous lust.

The ecstasy that there was torn from life
In wild delirium, in frantic pain,
In wanton recklessness returns to strain
The leash that holds the brooding dead from strife.

Cathedral bells and masses, hooded monks,
A leper's litany; the surging seas
Revolve and curve about the rounded knees,
And close and grapple with the prostrate trunks.

A mask emerges, green, with livid eyes
And bulbous lips; lean-cheeked, El Grecowise,
It nods above the orange-trees and throws
A shadow of its substance on the skies.

Martial: The Vacationist

Apollinaris skips away
When Rome becomes too hot:
He likes the beach at Formia
Where troubles are forgot.

There Thetis never says a word,
And yet her face is green,
And wrinkled by a gracious breeze
The swaying boughs between.

And flapper maids with purple fans
Refrigerate the air,
While widows walk upon the beach
With bobbed and powdered hair.

Apollinaris drops a line
Attached to hook and bait,
And leaning from a window-ledge
He gets a fish elate.

Apollinaris knows, dear lad,
That he has all the luck,
While you and I must stay at home
And pass along the buck.

From the Catullian Fount

I

You bid me tell, my Lesbia dear,
When I shall cease to love you!
How many kisses do you fear
Will satiate and cloy me here
By all the gods above you?
More than the grains of Libyan sand
Upon Cyrenian beaches,
From awful Ammon's monstrous dome
To great gray Battu's gilded tomb
Beyond the Grecian reaches.

II

My Lesbia says she loves me,
And no one else will wed;
My love is very suave and free,
And might take Jove instead!
Never trust what women swear
Unless they write it on the air.

III

If in pity you should grant me
Your wine-red lips to kiss and kiss,
The gods themselves would start to see
Three hundred thousand tithes of bliss.

But even then I should not cease!
No love can satiate such founts:
Far richer than the Golden Fleece
Our monstrous crop of kisses mounts.6

IV

Sirmio's greenness falls—
Petals of gale-blown flowers—
I have come from a city of walls
To dream in Sirmio's bowers.
I treasure floating lakes,
And the sand our huge sun cakes,
And the great sea when it breaks—
A place to waste the hours!
Pale green petals fall
Upon these glassy bowers,
And an endless, winding wall.

FRANK BELKNAP LONG, Jr.

The Darkling Tide

Previously Uncollected Poetry

THE DARKLING TIDE (Tsathoggua Press, September 1995)

Cover Illustration by Robert H. Knox

Introduction to THE DARKLING TIDE by Donald Sidney-Fryer

FLOTSAM AND JETSAM ON *THE DARKLING TIDE*

Reading and re-reading the poems of Frank Belknap Long (1901 - 1994) today during the mid-1990s, it is easy to perceive the qualities that must have attracted the considerable praise of such figures as diverse as George Sterling, John Masefield, Samuel Loveman, and even Arthur Machen himself. These qualities include imaginativeness, originality, craftsmanship, and especially the seemingly light but rarely trivial touch so characteristic of this poet. In short, it is good solid work worthy of extended perusal and contemplation. Belknap Long was only a young adult when his first collection appeared in 1926 as *A Man from Genoa and Other Poems*; and he was only a little older when his second collection appeared in 1935 as *The Goblin Tower*. When by reciprocal agreement, half a dozen years after the death of August Derleth in 1971 as the original editor-proprietor, Arkham House arranged with Belknap Long to republish in one volume the contents of the two earlier collections, the poet-author then in his mid-seventies apparently subjected the poems to some slight revision, and even discarded a few selections. The new volume appeared in 1977 as *In Mayan Splendor* as a singularly handsome little book with exceptionally beautiful illustrations by Stephen Fabian. Obviously such a republication of earlier work had left a considerable amount of other poems ungathered, including in this category a surprising number of later pieces in free verse as well as a small number of vignettes in prose.

Even after establishing a solid reputation as an original and all-around writer of imaginative fiction of diverse types—fantasy, science fiction, supernatural horror, &c.—Belknap Long still continued to regard himself primarily as a poet. Moreover, he took justifiable pride in his poetic output, and continued to turn out a rare piece of verse on occasion during the middle and then the latter part of his rather long life and career. His over-all output of poems would seem to be quite a bit less than one hundred titles, and—including his vignettes in prose—somewhere around seventy pieces. Whereas *In Mayan Splendor* gathered exactly forty selections (including his memorial sonnet to H. P. Lovecraft first published in 1938), there are still some thirty pieces or less remaining unharvested. These remnants Perry M. Grayson has collected into the present volume appropriately called *The Darkling Tide*, and including at least three notable poems that deal with, or touch on, the sea: *Innsmouth Revisited*, *Man Is the Sea's Child*, and *The Sea's Cold Blueness*. Furthermore, in gathering them into the present volume, Mr. Grayson has rendered a real service not only to the cause and reputation of the original poet-author himself but just as much to the aficionados and collectors of highly imaginative poetry. This is a type of poetry that unfortunately has become increasingly scarce, particularly as cast in the fixed forms but mutable figures of speech characteristic of the older prosody.

The survival of such poetry, generally rimed and metered, and often of quite an imaginative type, has become increasingly uncertain. In fact, it is possible that, at least as practiced by major poets, this kind of poetry may very well disappear completely, or almost so, in the next quarter or half of a century, if indeed it will even last that long. Nevertheless, it is part of a continuous tradition that in one shape or another goes back at least to the High Middle Ages, and possibly even to the ninth and tenth centuries of the Christian Era, to the revival of learning that took place under Alcuin at the court of Charlemagne during the eighth and ninth centuries at Aachen, or Aix-la-Chapelle, an over-all period that probably was distinguished most notably by the coronation of the Frankish ruler at Rome in December of 800 A.D. as Emperor of the West.

The first great efflorescence of this new poetic tradition (as distinguished from that of the ancient Greek and Roman world) manifested itself in the *chansons de geste* of the 1000s and 1100s, then in the metrical romances of the 1100s and 1200s (probably the first modern fiction), and concomitantly in the poems of the troubadours and trouvères of the same centuries, poems that the poets themselves characteristically sang, or hired other people to sing for them. The new tradition produced its greatest achievements in such diverse works as *La Chanson de Roland* (c. 1100), *Le Roman de la Rose* (c. 1235 and 1280), *The Divine Comedy* (completed in 1321), *The Canterbury Tales* (created in the last two decades of the 1300s), and then the sonnets and other love poems devised by Petrarch during the 1300s as inspired by the hopeless passion that he felt for Laura. (The preceding enumeration has no pretension to being complete, of course.) In these lyrics the spiritualized passion for the ideal and also unattainable—first developed and celebrated by the troubadours and trouvères, and always concentrated on the figure of a woman—found its culminating expression and apotheosis. In turn, the love poems of Petrarch would inspire countless lovers and poets throughout Europe not only during the Renaissance but even far beyond it.

This first great period of poetry created in the new languages that evolved after the collapse of the Western Roman Empire—poetry, moreover, that often was intensely and archetypally Romantic in feeling—we might designate for convenience, in the absence of other inclusive terms, after the dominant styles of architecture that came into existence during the Middle Ages: the Romanesque of the 1000's and 1100's, and the Gothic of the 1200's through the 1400's. Although not exact, the parallel between literature and architecture during this over-all 'Romanesco-Gothic' period is nevertheless close enough.

The same spirit animating this earliest Romantic efflorescence emerged again in the fantastic narratives in verse by such figures of the Renaissance (the 1400's and 1500's) as Ludovico Ariosto and Torquato Tasso, such narratives as *Orlando Furioso* (varying editions 1516-1532) and *Gerusalemme Liberata* (completed 1575, and published 1581). Such epic-romance-allegories as these had straightforwardly descended from the metrical romances of the 1100s and 1200s. The Romantic efflorescence of Ariosto, Tasso, and other poets found its ultimate expression in the last great poem of both the Middle Ages and the Renaissance, *The Faerie Queene* of Edmund Spenser (published 1590, 1596, and 1609). The same poetic fire that had burst forth in the Middle Ages, and that emerged again in the Renaissance, made its appearance possibly at its most powerful during the 1800s, the Romantic Century *par excellence*, but as a conscious artistic movement Romanticism really began in the late 1700's, and then continued on into the twentieth century long after the 1800's.

In English, of course, it includes all the great Romantic and Victorian poets: William Blake, Wordsworth, Coleridge, Keats, Shelley, Thomas Lovell Beddoes, Tennyson, Swinburne, &c. Needless to mention, great poets writing in almost all the European languages existed and flourished not only during the Middle Ages and the Renaissance but particularly during the 1800's. However, the modern Romanticism of such American poets as George Sterling, Nora May French, Clark Ashton Smith, Edna St. Vincent Millay, and Samuel Loveman, among many other figures, occurred largely during the first fourth, third, or half of the twentieth century, and also thus included the early collections of Belknap Long, which tied in another form during the second half of the same century. The major part of the poems in verse and vignettes in prose, collected here for the first time during the 1990's, goes back to the 1920's and 1930's, and includes quite a few beautiful, enchanting, and otherwise remarkable effusions. These lyrics directly remind us of the idealistic and imaginative type of poetry that was predominantly characteristic of the first fourth or third of the 1900's in the U.S.A.

Why has the survival of such poetry as these lyrics become uncertain, that is, in terms of an ongoing tradition that is not just alive but flourishing? The answer is unequivocal, and comes from the alternate poetic tradition (often burningly Romantic in feeling as well) that has developed in the last century and a half, originating in the U.S.A. out of the general American poet's need to convey an experience of life differing from that of Europe. The poetic tradition that we have just sketched, involving as it does both rime and meter, we might call for convenience the Mediaeval Syndrome, arising as it did in the early Middle Ages and lasting through all the centuries since then on into our own modern period. When the Old World settled and colonized the New World, the emigrants naturally brought with them the literary traditions and forms of the Old World in the various European languages. However, these forms, genres and themes ultimately could only go so far in adapting to the lifestyles of the New World, and it was inevitable that new forms and modes of literature would arise, which they did, of course.

It was none other than Walt Whitman (born 1819) who began the poetic revolution in the mid-1800s with his *Leaves of Grass*, first published in 1855. This collection he revised and enlarged through nine successive editions before his death in 1892. Whitman's poetic resolution would ultimately exert an enormous influence throughout North, Central, and South America, as well as throughout Europe, whether directly or indirectly. T. S. Eliot and Ezra Pound at least in English renewed and continued this revolution in their own idiosyncratic manner, particularly in the 1920's and 1930's. In turn, highly visible in the 1950's and 1960's, such figures as Allen Ginsberg, Kenneth Rexroth, and Lawrence Ferlinghetti, among many other poets primarily centered in the San Francisco Bay Area (the so-called Beatniks of the Beat Generation), renewed and continued the same revolution in their own idiosyncratic but inclusively democratic manner, thus restoring the impetus to its original source in Whitman. The Beatniks ultimately exerted even greater influence than Eliot and Pound.

In this new poetic development—and we are dead serious on this point—we should make considerable allowance for the equally new tradition of sung poetry represented by rock and roll music and its leading practitioners, such groups above all as the Beatles, the Rolling Stones, the Grateful Dead, the Jefferson Airplane/Starship, the Doors, &c., especially prominent and influential during the 1960's and 1970's. Indeed, Jim Morrison (or, in full, James Douglas Morrison), the lead singer of the Doors, as a modern Romantic poet (in feeling, if not in terms of literary form), may be seen as the equivalent in the twentieth century of such English Romantic poets as Byron, Keats, and Shelley. The result of all these changes and innovations is that, almost universally, poets today write in prose of extraordinary variety, but still in prose, the ultimate heritage from Whitman. Much of the new poetry since the mid-1900s has become, alas! even more autobiographical than it ever was even during the time of the English and American Romantics of the 1800's; and although some of it inevitably remains obscure, most of it is relatively accessible, at least with some serious attention.

Since the 1950's, especially in the San Francisco Bay Area, a major poetic rebirth has taken place, inspired in part by the public readings there of the great Welsh poet Dylan Thomas on tour in the U.S.A. during 1952; and this poetic rebirth has developed its own autochthonous tradition of poetry publicly performed, sometimes accompanied by music such as jazz. Another result of all these changes and innovations, and just as important, is that poetry has become accessible again to the average person, and thus concerned with the recognizable dysfunctions, problems, and joys of everyday life and existence. Although some of it remains obscure, it is today for the most part no longer arcane, or but rarely so, and rarely is it sublime. A notable exception may be cited in the extraordinary visions and effusions of the great American Surrealistic poet Philip Lamantia, who continues in a number of exceptional ways, both subtle and overt, many of the more arcane traditions represented by the epochal poetry of Clark Ashton Smith, no mean accomplishment.

The restoration of relatively accessible poetry to people at large, through the medium of public performance as much as through that of the printed page, compensates perhaps for the loss of the incisive type of speech or expression, the loss of the Romantic afflatus, no less than that of the Romantic style of imagination, all of which were so richly purveyed by metrical poetry from the Romanesque period onward. Renewed with undeniable splendor during the Renaissance and then later during the Romantic Century, the tradition of Romantic poetry is yet somehow alive after so many poetic revolutions and counter-revolutions, as witness these hitherto ungathered Romantic lyrics and other more modern effusions by Frank Belknap Long. Who knows but that we may be looking for the last time at the last of the last as we pick up and peruse this collection?! We could be wrong, and we hope that we are indeed wrong. If in fact we are looking at the last of the last, then let us cherish these remnants, and let us revel in the fun, fancy, and lyric expansiveness of a young poet who reached his coming of age just a little over seventy years ago.

–Donald Sidney-Fryer, Sacramento, California
the Fourth of July, 1995

The Migration of Birds

FROM *THE UNITED AMATEUR* (MARCH 1922)

In the Autumn of the year, when the decay of things is imminent, and when the face of the moon is as pallid and bloodless as the visage of a corpse, I ofttimes sit by a little window opening on the summer sea and watch the migration of birds. They come from all parts of the world, these birds, aye, even from that ultimate dim Thule which the Romans knew but dared not mention, and they bring with them the strange, pungent odors and secret essences of distant lands.

The parakeets are the first to arrive. Their bills are black, their plumage iridescent, and they scream in the moonlight. They are talkative, vulgar, aristocratic. How I hate them! They are like spoilt children crying over a broken doll. But they tell me something of the equator, something of red and gold on blue, something of naked black men sitting cross-legged and pensive under the hot tropical sun, something of huge, waving palms and gigantic Lianas, and something of the turbulent, green, ever-restless Spanish main, and so I tolerate them. And you would too, O my reader, because Dreams are of more value than oriental jewels.

But the parakeets pass quickly. They dislike our cold northern clime, and pine for the delights of the soft South. Their breasts are full of vague longings and inarticulate, unborn desires; and in their eyes there is a vision of other places, far, outlying immensities of land, and ocean. And so they pass quickly.

And then in the pale twilight of an ancient November eve come flocking the swarms of flamingoes. They are pinky pale and older than the flood. For always have flamingoes come up from the South in the Spring, and returned in the Autumn; and if you have not seen them, you are a fool. The flamingoes are wise with the wisdom of ages, but they are eternally young. You remember that glorious fountain of youth and gold which Ponce de Leon sought in the dawn of the world? The flamingoes have found it, and every year they return to bathe and gambol in its mystic waters. Every year they sink their great, pale plumes in its gentle waters, and arise refreshed and reincarnated. But the flamingoes also long for the tropics, and for the flush of dawn on peaks divine. And so they follow the parakeets to the warm South.

The geese are cold and unemotional, and arouse no visions. They have always suffered from ennui, and the world is little with them. Perhaps in their youth they have tasted of many pleasures, and now suffer from the boredom of satiety. But they cast not a glance at my little window, but with inflated pinions and half-closed, sleepy eyes pass quietly over the laughing waters.

The last to arrive are the birds of ebony. The moonlight plays sadly upon their black plumage, and is seen reflected in their great, pale yellow eyes. How strange the moonlight looks when seen in their sad, watery, yellow eyes. They are the birds of ill-omen forever croaking Nevermore. And it is a fitting end. Let us pull down the heavy black shade, and retire from the window. The migrations are over, and the cold sere winter is at hand. Let us light a little fire, and dream by the fireside. Let us dream of the equator, of the warm South, of the sunny, of the happy South. Yes, let us dream.

Young Frank Belknap Long, H. P. Lovecraft & James F. Morton at the Edgar Allan Poe cottage, New York, 1922.

At the Home of Poe

TO H. P. LOVECRAFT
FROM *THE UNITED AMATEUR* (MAY 1922)

The home of Poe! It is like a fairy dwelling, a gnomic palace built of the ether of dreams. It is tiny and delicate and lovely, and replete with memories of sere leaves in November and of lilies in April. It is a castle of vanished hopes, of dimly-remembered dreams, of sad memories older than the deluge. The dead years circle slowly and solemnly around its low white walls, and clothe it in a mystic veil of unseen tears. And many marvelous stories could this quaint little old house tell, many weird and cryptic stories of him of the Raven hair, and high, pallid brow, and sad, sweet face, and melancholy mien; and of the beloved Virginia, that sweet child of a thousand magic visions, child of the lonesome, pale-gray latter years, child of the soft and happy South. And how the dreamer of the spheres must have loved this strange little house. Every night the hollow boards of its porch must have echoed to his footfall, and every morn the great rising sun must have sent its rays through the little window, and bathed the lovely tresses of the dream-child in mystical yellow. And perhaps there was laughter within the walls of that house, laughter and merriment and singing. But we know that the Evil One came at last, the grim humorless specter who loves not beauty, and is not of this world. And we know that the house of youth and of love became a house of death, and that memories bitter as the tears of a beautiful woman assailed the dreamer within. And at last he himself left that house of mourning and sought solace among the stars. But the house remains a vision out of a magical book; a thing seen darkly as in a looking-glass; but lovely beyond the dreams of mortals, and ineffably sad.

Edgar Allan Poe (1809 - 1849)

Flowers of Iniquity

FROM *HOME BREW* (JULY 1922)

There is a whispering among the tombs.
An unclad woman, old and wrinkled, sits on an antique sepulcher, and combs her disheveled yellow hair.
A green snake coils lazily around her thin, reed-like legs.
The woman stops combing, and sings to the serpent.
Her voice is that of a siren, low and vibrant, and lovely
beyond the dream of mortals.
The snake, fascinated, writhes slowly upward, and finally stretches forth its smiling, cynical lips to be kissed.
The serpent and the woman unite in a long, lingering embrace.
The serpent swoons with ecstasy, and at length, it dies.
The woman sings on.

* * *

The lighted caravans pass slowly over the desert.
There is a sound of revelry within.
Without the jackals and panthers confide to the stars their
immedicable woe.
Suddenly a cry, shrill and terse, and replete with horror, issues from one of the illuminated vehicles.
An Arab descends, and flees screaming
He is devoured by the panthers and jackals

A woman looks out and laughs
The panthers and jackals flee.

* * *

They looked into each other's eyes, and smiled.
They were happy, these two.
Even Nero, the emperor of all the world would never know such love as theirs.
Neither would Petronius.
But they had not counted upon the wars.
The sad news found them in each others arms on a great marble portico overlooking the soft Campania.
'I must go, my beloved!' he wailed. 'It would never do to disobey the Purple One!'
Without a word she bent, and plucked a rose from the innumerable thorns.
'Take it, O my adored one!' she pleaded, holding it toward him.
He seized the proffered flower, and passionately pressed it to his lips.
But it had turned into a snake and bit him.
He did not go to the wars.

* * *

He fell madly in love with the old stone gods.
He wrote long erotic poems to them, and even had their
effigies erected in his study.
One day as he was passing under the marble bust of
Aphrodite he became indiscreet, and addressed the goddess in
platitudes. 'Do you love me as I love you, O fair daughter of the immortals?' he asked.
Receiving no reply, he entirely forgot himself.
'Thy lips are like pomegranates!' he declared
The marble bust of Aphrodite fell, and hit him upon the head.
He has since lost all interest in archaeology.

? ? ? IT IS FOR YOU TO ANSWER, WILL HAYS ? ? ?
"THE DEBAUCH OF THE MOVIES" Page Three
25¢
HOME BREW
PEPPY STORIES - PUNGENT JESTS - PIQUANT GOSSIP
JULY
1922
TOOTSIE
Flapper Commandments—42
FLOWERS OF INIQUITY—23
Did She Fall or Was She Pushed?—81
BRINGING UP FATHER
AMERICA'S ZIPPIEST POCKET MAGAZINE
EDITED BY MISSUS and MISTER GEORGE JULIAN HOUTAIN

Ingenue

FROM *THE NATIONAL AMATEUR* (MAY 1923)

Ingenue, why do you persist in starting at the loquacious visage of the dawn? Think of the ironical perturbations which that Medusa face occasioned your amazingly lean grandfather. Be agile. Flee with me into the absurd twilight of an inebriate forest, and we shall walk arm in arm through a lugubrious carnival of burning cypresses. It is well to defy conventions, and I cannot believe that you regret the color of your hair. See even now pituitous willows enfold us, and we tread gingerly over the crisp and placid leaves—we pensively wander among grinning oaks, and joyous vegetation. Do not be disturbed by the hoarse and rasping wail of ebullient nightingales, or the sheer bad taste of orthodox ravens letting out hallelujahs. There are many things to chaunt of as we deliriously romp among the fantastic shadows. A modest corpse grins disenchantingly from yon piebald oak, and an eyeless madman points with serried tarsus toward the poisonous East. The pellucid mist insinuates itself into the confidence of the colossal trees, and tears savagely at our damp and cowering raiment. It were wiser to flee the mist than to divest ourselves of our raiment. An indigent snail creeps warily over the protruding pates of dead men prematurely bald. Courage! The tarns themselves will enfold us should we despair of our insane existence.

In the ultramarine of your eyes I can discern sunken galleons which despairing suitors have launched there in seeking to penetrate the iciness of your reserve. In the Gmelin blue of your eyes I behold the phthisic countenances of spineless Amitabhas who idiotically seek pyrotechnics amidst the rotting carcasses. In the lovely lapis lazuli of your torpid eyes I glimpse the bulbous monstrosity which my egoism warns me not to acknowledge.

In the fastness of your hair I lose myself dreaming of forests on stilts. Amid the voluptuous aridity of your springy hair I gnaw at transparent microisms who indulgently pander to my avidity. In the hieratic wilderness of your sumptuous hair I am often aware of seemingly irresponsible globules wandering aimlessly among the withering golden strands.

Look! At our feet a blue pool mocks our naiveté, and the wrinkles on its hypocritical face defy analysis. Infamous ixiolirions blossom upon its withering banks, and teasingly taunt a dozen iridescent toads, who at this very moment are insensately glaring at us with their oneiroscopic eyes. A palsied jaguar intimates his intention of destroying himself because of the unthinkable stupidity of irrational Elaeagnaceae. We must not linger. Do you know that I have spotted Pythons as long as laucous Dugongs? I am sure that the cynical yellow lobsters will triumph, and that the indignant jellyfish will crawl away through the forest to die of gerontition on the eburneous shores of angry silver streams. And they were so beautiful with their audacious tentacles eternally sucking at stunted effluvia. I wish Habakkuk could have seen them. The lobsters are austere and cruel, and do not appeal to the aesthetic sensibilities of the disillusioned dilettante.

Your lips are irrelevantly enticing. I cannot believe they were made to order. There is a passionate originality about them which is unmistakable. They are free from insane imperfections. And yet they have a distressing habit of sardonically smiling at my fumbling indiscretions. They are notoriously lacking in a sense of propriety. Their method of attack is incisive, and one is often taken unawares. But I shall venture to state that they are amusingly exact in punishing premeditated assiduity.

Come, let us romp and ramble over the laughing meadows, and watch the lascivious sun stain elongated reaches of weeping oats a delicious citrine. Tiny tintinnabulations arise from the reeking eelgrass, and warn us that we have ventured too far. Oh! I have dreamed of these things on the hollow edges of damp pantries, but to skip and gambol with one of your charm and amiability through the unexpected morn is more than I could have hoped for. Delirious dreams settle themselves complacently upon the white plain, and I ecstatically kiss the blue nails of your pink and bloated hand. Love itself perpetrates a slow salaam while I whisper to you the necromantic secrets of modernity. Let us bear our cross.

But we must tread divergent paths. I have marveled at your complaisance, which was but pity for my madness. And you alone are sane. O my dear child, how shall I ever make you understand me? I prefer cannabis, and aromatic herbs to cigars and coffee. I prefer the golden sands of incredible beaches and the clear cry of the pathetic penguin at dawn to the cinema. I detest wigs, and love to wade knee-deep into the indigo of refulgent seas. Let us kiss, and part. You have socks to darn, and I must straddle the sun, and ride wildly across the mad and screaming heavens. Adieu!

Felis

FROM *THE CONSERVATIVE* NO. 13 (JULY 1923)

Oh, how delightful it is to stroke the sinuous hair of felicitous cats. Long, long ago I discovered that these happy creatures know more than Adam our father because they have never been tempted by the evil one, have never eaten of the forbidden fruit and have never fallen. I know that in their great, tearless, seductive eyes there lurk sinister secrets, preincarnate hieroglyphics which only the gods can fathom, secrets and signs which portend nothing but evil for man. And they are immortal; you cannot kill them. When the tiny sphere which certain weary seers have agreed to call the earth, for lack of a better name, shall have permitted itself to become cold through sheer ennui there shall yet remain the cats. They are immortal and shall live always, even as the old stone gods, even as the voluptuous Venus, even as the albino and implacable Delphic Apollo. Long have I studied them, and I have become, in a degree, their slave. They have begun to exercise an unholy fascination over me and have even stolen into my dreams, into the secret chambers of my fancy. I shall always see them now, whenever I dream, large, and sinewy and soft with prismatic eyes, scintillating eyes, vacillating eyes, eyes green and blue, and pale, washed-out yellow, like the mournful orbs of the melancholy Kakue bird of Paraguay who possesses the immortal soul of a negress. And in my dreams they climb over my arms and legs and purr and whine disconsolately. And when I reach out, fascinated, and smooth their long fur I experience a joy at once profound and awful *because their fur is soft and burns my fingers.*

There is something *outré* about their fur. I have seen great waste places entirely inhabited by cats. I have seen cats of all colors, of all shades, of all hues, and of every shape and size. I have seen shrunken cats and cats with elephantiasis and deformed and misshapen and dwarfed cats. I have seen cats that could talk and cats that could laugh and, yes, I have actually seen a cat who could dance. But whenever I dream of cats I see the spiced mummy of some august Pharaoh, or a skeleton rider carrying a scythe riding furiously around an ever widening circle or a radiant corpse swinging gracefully under a cloudless blue sky. When I walk the streets of our great cities I am haunted by cats. I see them everywhere, behind smooth glass of costly limousines, on street corners, in the languid eyes of women, by deserted waterfronts, in the smoke of a man's pipe, on top of tall buildings, down dark and unfrequented alleys, and in the pale yellow light of the city's gas lamps. Someday I shall drown in a sea of cats. I shall go down, smothered by their embraces, feeling their warm breath upon my face, gazing into their large eyes, hearing in my ears their soft purring. I shall sink lazily down through oceans of fur, between myriads of claws, clutching innumerable tails and I shall surrender my wretched soul to the selfish and insatiable god of felines.

H. P. Lovecraft holds Felis, Frank Belknap Long's cat.

To Felis, Frank Belknap Long's Cat by H. P. Lovecraft

I

Little Tiger, burning bright
With a subtle Blakeish light,
Tell what visions have their home
In those eyes of flame and chrome!
Children vex thee—thoughtless, gay—
Holding when thou wouldst away:
What dark lore is that which thou,
Spitting, mixest with thy meow?

II

Haughty Sphinx, whose amber eyes
Hold the secrets of the skies,
As thou ripplest in thy grace,
Round the chairs and chimney-place,
Scorn on thy patrician face:
Hiss not harsh, nor use thy claws
On the hand that give applause—
Good-will only doth abide
In these lines at Christmastide!

The Rebel (1924 Version)

FROM *THE UNITED AMATEUR* (MAY 1924)

But when they came and whispered, "He is dead!"
I somehow knew his dreams would never stay.
Within a graceless and a chastened head:
His golden thoughts were made for seas of fay!
He hated cities and their iron marts;
He longed for palms against a sunset sky;
His only friends were lads with sea-tamed hearts;
He loved tall masts and great ships scudding by.

For there are men who never sail in ships,
Who cannot bide the thought of any land;
As children they awake with parted lips,
Amazed by endless leagues of sunlit sand—
Elusive souls who slip from dusty streets
To Western Islands with the zest of Keats.

["The Rebel" was revised by Long after its initial appearance in *The United Amateur*. This is the first version. -PMG]

The Rebel

But when they came & whispered, "He is dead!"
I somehow knew his dreams would never stay
Within a graceless & a chastened head:
His golden thoughts were made for seas of fay!
He hated cities and their crowded marts;
He longed for palms against a sunset sky;
His only friends were men with sea-tamed hearts;
He loved tall masts & great ships scudding by.

For there are men who never sail in ships
Who cannot bide the thought of any land;
As children they awake with parted lips
Amazed by endless leagues of sunlit sand—
Elusive souls who slip from dusty streets
To Western Islands with the zest of Keats.

F. B. Long, Jr.
United Amateur
May 1924

Autographed manuscript of "The Rebel"

O Is There Aught in Wine and Ships?

FROM *THE OVERLAND MONTHLY* (NOV. 1926)

Beneath the changing Roman moon
Catullus glides on nimble feet:
Above his head the roses wake;
Upon his brow the air is sweet.

The city breathes a fragrance out
And dreams upon its silver hills:
Above his head the roses break
And bloom upon the windowsills.

He does not let his fancy stray
To cities lying deep in dust:
Above his head the roses bloom;
And Lesbia's lips are red as rust.

And Lesbia's lips are good to kiss!
O is there aught in wine and ships
And gold and frankincense and myrrh
As sweet as Lesbia's painted lips?

Let Virgil sing of gods and kings
And islands in the farthest seas:
The myrtles and the roses wake,
And twine about her wanton knees.

Beneath the changing Roman moon
Catullus glides on nimble feet:
Above his head the roses bloom;
Upon his brow the air is sweet.

Did You Write Lovecraft?

FROM A DEC. 1928 LETTER TO H. P. LOVECRAFT

Ah, did you see Lovecraft plain?
And did he stop and write to you?
And did you write to him again
How strange it seems, and new!

I passed a moor[I] with a name of its own
And a use in the world no doubt
Yet a hand's breadth of it[II] shines alone
O'er the low miles round about

For there I pick upon the heather
And there I put inside my breast
A moulted feather, an eagle's[III] feather—
Well I forget the rest...

Notes
[I]Providence, R.I.
[II]10 Barnes Street
[III]Roman

[This poem was previously untitled. The footnotes are FBL's own. -PMG]

Dear Howard:
CONGRATULATIONS! No doubt you will appear between Cabell and Sherwood Anderson! A chap here who writes extensively for the cigar-stand magazines assures me that you are now an established author, and that you will have no difficulty whatever in selling stuff to Harpers and The Atlantic. It was inevitable that the simple country gentleman without literary interests or pretensions should have become the infant terrible of the status quo. Thank Pitrarcha I have preserved all of your correspondence.

"Ah, did you once see Lovecraft plain?
And did he stop and write to you?
And did you write to him again?
How strange it seems, and new!

I passed a moor[I] with a name of its own
And a use in the world no doubt (?)
Yet a hand's breadth of it[II] shines alone
O'er the low miles round about.

For there I picked up on the heather
And there I put inside my breast
A moulted feather, an eagle's[III] feather –
Well, I forget the rest

Notes.
I – Providence R.I.
II – 10 Barnes Street
III – Roman

I hope they don't discover that you are in the habit of celebrating black mass three times a day, and that you occasionally eat infants raw!

Did you describe your exploits in the Greek army in the sketch you sent O'Brien? And did you mention the Dunn Slinglish incident – how you caned Slinglish and kicked him downstairs? I hope you haven't neglected this priceless opportunity to romanticize yourself – think of the glorious little extensions of mere prosaic actuality one could introduce into a sketch of this sort. I should have certainly referred to my royal Spanish ancestry and I should have described the look of amazement and indignation on the face of Lord Cecil when I pulled his nose

To FBL on His Birthday by H. P. Lovecraft

Belknap, how quick does time again
Draw forth the tributary strain,
And move Old Age afresh to greet
The milestone pass'd by youthful feet!
Have I thy birthday rightly heard—
Is this indeed thy twenty-third?
Sure, infant genius swift is nurs'd
To manhood's prime, in wisdom vers'd!
But tho' thy mind be thus mature,
Let boyish fancy linger pure,
Nor with each mounting natal day
Cast innocence and grace away;
Coarseness reject, corruption spurn,
From subtle sophists proudly turn,
And keep, intact in every part,
The wonder of a Virgin Heart!

The Beautiful City

FROM *LEAVES* NO. 1 (SUMMER 1937)

Immense it stands upon the desert's rim
No strident city torn by violent wars
But lovelier than evening's gorgeous stars
And friendlier than maid or seraphim:
All day within its walls the people dance
Or play upon the silvery bassoon;
And there are runners straighter than a lance
And clean-eyed lovers laughing at the moon.

The camel-drivers seek it and are glad
When its dear name is whispered over fires;
Its golden walls and changeless, foam-white spires
Cheer lonely tramps and kings whose hearts are sad:
Its bells are heard on all the seven seas
And worshippers draw near it on their knees.

Futility

FROM *LEAVES* NO. 2 (WINTER 1938)

It doesn't matter what we do
For when we die we'll rot,
And worms will through our livers crawl
And on our gizzards trot.

Adjuration

FROM *FIRE AND SLEET AND CANDLELIGHT*, EDITED BY AUGUST DERLETH (1961)

It has been rumored that there are
Glacial Splendors
In the dark of the moon;
Great winds blowing,
And blue-ice mountains
As resplendent as a child's
Spinning top
In the wonder-world of
The very young,
When every new toy
Has the magic of circus elephants,
Giraffes with a fine gloss,
A ringmaster with jointed limbs
And a Mechano-set.
On Mars, too—and Venus;
Grail-bright splendors,
Lakes Darien-new,
Titan crests
Coiling into foam.
Rejoice then and be bold!
Ride the wild stallions
At the Atom's core
Be poets, visionaries without guilt!

Has it not been said:
'He who stands
At the precipice's edge
Must have a god's strength,
A god's bold wisdom?'

The New Adam

FROM *FIRE AND SLEET AND CANDLELIGHT*

On the lowlands where the angular shadows
Blend with blooms of intricate design
A beauty Euclidean hides the veld spore
Of the great beasts, and the attentive ear
Must strain to catch the far-off trumpet roar
Of herds of angry pachyderm, half-maddened
By the devious barbs of hunters eight in line.
On the heights that ancient savagery
Fades to nothingness. The blue alone survives,
Infinite in depth, and there the lives
Of all the space-born create an imagery
Light-year strange ... there build new hives
For cosmic bees, the honey-gatherers of Eternity.

It Is Not Only the Dead

FROM FIRE AND SLEET AND CANDLELIGHT

It is not only the dead
Who walk in graveyards,
Where the mildew
Glows like silver talc,
And the talk is of
Milady's teacups
And Stratford'sWhite-throated swan.
The unborn walk there too;
The Atom's offspring,
Mongolian idiots,
Tongue-tied mutants,
And wild horsemen
Of the coastal plains,
Clad in the skins
Of animals,
And dismounted to rest
Where the mottled skulls
Cluster thickly.

Innsmouth Revisited

FROM *XENOPHILE* NO. 18 (OCT. 1975)

I knew I would find him,
If at all,
Where the black wharves rose
Above the darkling tides,
And the crooked houses stood
Row on row,
As silent as weed-nibbling carp
In a stagnant pool.
I could hear the silence as I walked,
A terrible absence of sound,
Lapping at the barnacle-encrusted piles.
I saw him at last,
Standing apart and alone,
Stiller than the stillest shadow,
Until he turned.
'Belknapius!' he cried,
'What are you doing here?'
'It is your Innsmouth,' I replied.
'You created it, but now—'
'But now?'
'It haunts us all. A legacy imperishable.
Your gift to dreamers everywhere.
A sable legacy, like Edgar's,
But sublime.'

'I have grown weary of it,' he said,
'After all these years—'
He straightened as he spoke
And gazed skyward,
Where the mist-hidden moon
Had lost its way.
'I have found another Innsmouth,' he said.
'Far beyond the universe of stars.
I never could have dreamed—'
All at once a haziness enveloped him,
And I had to strain
To catch his words.
'Look for me there, Belknapius,
In aeons remote from ours,
Look for me there.'
Then he was gone.

Photomontage of FBL and HPL
by Andrea Bonazzi

Man Is the Sea's Child

FROM *OMNIUMGATHIUM*, ED. BY JONATHAN BACON AND STEVE TROYANOVICH (1976)

Man is the sea's child
Spawned in her dark-bright womb:
At first a tiny stirring
In warm primordial ooze,
In cliff rocks, in tidal pools
Transformed by Solar chemistry
And cosmic rays
Dark eons of stirring
Feeling the imminent coming
Of something more complex,
But knowing only
A flagelliform stirring.
Spores green-gold, glinting
In naked sunlight
Feeling death-life
A greediness, a restlessness.
Hungry mouths still unformed
Seeking moisture, nutrient fluids
Knowing the agony
Of being alive
The primal agony
Before the coming of Mind

Knowing the rapture
In every jellied part
Agony-rapture, life-death
Not one, but two
Two now, in a wild blending
The great mystery
Of fission-sex
Half-pain, half-ecstasy
Mindless still
But all Mind
In un-Mind
Then up, up, up
Amoeba, jellyfish,
Iridescent sea worm,
Trilobite, sea scorpion
Who shall say
How each in turn
Became Lords of Life
For a hundred million years?
Sea-swimmers with no backbone,
Sea-swimmers armor plated
And spined like hedgehogs
Fishes, reptiles,
Amphibians, Man
Man the sea-child
Cradled in her dark-bright womb
Massive-browed, cave-dwelling
Sea-singer and rune-maker
Bison-painter, pyramid builder
World creator and world destroyer
Man is the sea's child
Enraptured still by the bright tides,
Enraptured by the music and the wonder

Of breaking waves, high crested,
Curling into foam.

The Necronomicon – John Dee's Translation

FROM *CRYPT OF CTHULHU* NO. 23 (ST. JOHN'S EVE 1984)

(Retranslated into slightly more modern phrase patterns here and there, but without the slightest departure from the original text otherwise.)

Paragraphs Seven and Eight, Page 30, Book Three

It must not be thought that the powers capable of the greatest wickedness appear to us in the form of repellant familiars, and other, closely related demons. They do not. Small, visible demons are merely the effluvia which those vast forms of destructiveness have left in Their wake-skin scrapings and even more tenuous shreds of evil that attach themselves to the living like leeches from some great slain leviathan of the deep that has wreaked havoc on a hundred coastal cities before plunging to its death with a thousand hurled harpoons quivering in its flesh.

For the mightiest powers there can be no death and the hurled harpoons inflict, at most, surface injuries which heal quickly. I have said before and I shall say again until my tardily earned wisdom is accepted by my brethren as fact-in confronting that which has always been and always will be a master of magic can know only self-reproach and despair if he mistakes a temporary victory for one that he can never hope permanently to win.

–Frank Belknap Long

(Who refuses to discuss how these few lines came into his possession.)

John Dee (1527 - 1608)

The Sea's Cold Blueness

FROM *FANTASY & TERROR* NO. 3 (1984)

The sea's cold blueness is by night
In so deep a chill encompassed
The shark fins seem to cut through the water
Into the heart of darkness
Like the scalpel of an unskilled surgeon
Blundering, blundering his way
Toward an aorta blood-sullied,
The sea's cold blueness
I affirm to be not without beauty
Its caverns an inscrutable Mandarin's
Toyshop wonder of cordage, compasses,
The skulls of brave sailors,
Octopi with the eyes of demons,
And shadows of coral reefs enpurpled.
To travel far in the night sea
You have only to don
Your best skin outfit
And breast the tides with lungs inflated,
Eternity your goal.

Medieval Palimpsest Fragment, AD 1165

FROM *FANTASY & TERROR* NO. 5 (1985)

In the long, cold corridors
Bare of all adornment
Solemnity is our only shield
Gone are the battle plumes
And the shining lances
Dust-cluttered, and spirited away
Into oblivion
Those proud plumes, purple and gold,
Had a longer day
Now we must be quick and decisive
Harsh and neat
Keep Death in a dust-proof casket
Life on a short, firm leash
Life more with us
Like a dog well-trained
Turn right, turn left
Accompanying each turn
With a tug on the leash
To bring Life up short
Life and ourselves
Dog and master

We must tolerate no nonsense
For Life must not envy Death.

To a Friend

FROM *FANTASY MACABRE* NO. 5 (1985)

To a friend
Who Felt He Was Growing Old,
On His Forty-Third Birthday

Congratulations on your forty-third
An age when I, without a word,
Listened to the woodland chimes
Saw dancing nymphs and piping Pans
With every dawn still brightly glowing,
The future still beyond all knowing.

Prophecy

FROM *FANTASY MACABRE* NO. 6 (1985)

If the great thunders
Pass skyward
,Taking with them}
All weed-choked gravestones,
Granite edifices,
Towers electronic,
And books opened by mistake
In the dark of the human mind,
By torment obsessed
Then will still remain,
An afterglow of Lovers,
Entwined on golden sands,
Sitting by quiet streams
And walking hand in hand
Through enchanted woodlands
Eternities remote,
From the Big Mushroom.

Rufus (Catullus)

FROM *CRYPT OF CTHULHU* NO. 42 (1986)

Rufus is worse than a ghoul in his sin,
He walks in the graveyard merely to win
From each opened grave one infamous meal,
His meat from each carcass, he bends low to steal,
And is beaten to death by the horrors within.

H. P. Lovecraft

FROM *WEIRD TALES* (JUNE 1938)

The many who perceive in you a glass
Held steadily against the outer dark,
Where Memphian shadows throng, and glories pass,
Illumined by the Eternal's fitful spark,
Glimpse but one facet of a wondrous light,
That fell resplendently on Earth's harsh shores,
And shed a radiance on the Spirit's flight,
That turned the priests of Mammon from our doors.

Beyond high mountain peaks your vision soared;
Across the glacial green which links the world,
Of ageless dreaming with the night's unfurled;
And eon-wide pinions by the blind abhorred.
Sublimer beauty* never dwelt with Poe,
Or walked with Shelley in the white dawn's glow.

*Long later changed this line to read "Sublimer insight never dwelt with Poe," during public recitals of this poem.

FBL and HPL in New York circa 1931

A Matter of Perspective

FROM *THE WOLVERINE* (DEC. 1920)

I am old and weary. I have drained the cup to its last drop. My youth is spent, my ambition dead. No longer do the hot coals of desire glow within me; no longer do I feel the impulse to accomplish and achieve. My blood has grown sluggish and my mind has become fogged. I have loved much, felt much, seen much; but my day is past. Alas, I shall be thirty tomorrow!

I am young, and overflowing with the zest and zeal of youth. I feel within me the strength of Samson and the ambition of Napoleon. I have scarce tasted of life's joys; I know nothing of the real pleasures of existence. Everything lies before me. My way is open. My path is clear. Beautiful maidens beckon me; strange mystic climes bid me wonder on their shores and pick rich fruit from their vines. Like a little child I reach forth my hands and pluck these treasures, and lo! my desire becomes greater than ever, and I glory in my endless enthusiasm and power to enjoy. I shall be sixty tomorrow!

Unhappiness

FROM *THE WOLVERINE* (DEC. 1922)

Even the moon, knowing how unhappy were the poor children of genius, wept tears of blood, and while her beautiful face was veiled in compassion, I left the sinister world of crowned mediocrities and wandered among the tombs. And among the immemorial bones of great men I found again the resplendent dreams and vision of my childhood. But when the gods saw me toying with joyous fancies older than the deluge they became angry, and swore that I should never again revisit the lovely scenes of my melancholy but mortal youth. So they shut me up in a great sea sepulcher, in a titan cave not far from the ever restless, ever heaving Spanish Main, where only the dimly heard waves brought me memories and visions of other times, and of other places. But no light from heaven penetrated into the unfathomable recesses of that great gray vault, and the unreverberate darkness oppressed my soul, and I sought solace in dreams of her who would ever again grow limp and warm in my arms with love. I dreamed of the beloved Rosa Belle who passed away with the tapers, many eons, many eternities, many lustra ago, and I called out her name that I might glory in the self-torment which the mere sound of the resonant syllables forced upon me. But when I sought to envisage the fair one I failed because of the numberless incubi, succubi, unhappy shades and little daemons that accompanied her spirit. And at length, crying out to the gods and Satan that I had been wronged, and that all of the morning beauty of the world had been taken from me I found my heart with a knife of gold, and surrendered my wretched soul to the Evil One. And I am now but a shade weeping with the pallid moon, a disconsolate phantom crying my incommunicable woe to the pale stars, a dream child eternally damned, eternally and immutably damned.

Sandaris

FROM *THE TRYOUT* (MAY 1925)

It was on a red dawn, when the mist lay like a wounded silver dragon in the valley that Sandaris awoke and heard the distant tinkling of sheep bells on far mountains above deserted vineyards. The last star glimmered faintly in the pale morning sky and Sandaris wondered why the star had delayed so long its fading and why the red dawn had not crept more rapidly upon it and dissolved it in a blaze of ruddy light. To Sandaris the simplest sounds and sights of morning were a hallowed mystery, and he speculated glamorously concerning the whyfor of the coming in of the day and slow, meditative withdrawal of the night with its dreams of ineffable sea-strange cities. As he lay coiled in golden drowsihood beneath a chestnut burr Sandaris sent his dreams on far, holy journeys, but he could not forget, even in his dreams, that he was an ugly, impure satyr, and he knew that he could never embark upon the glad and disastrously sanctified quest of the Sangrail. And yet the hard, indissolvable beauty of the uncorrupted vessel won his thoughts from all earthly attachments and although the grail could never rightly be his, he dreamed of it night and day.

And he often knew a desire to laugh and grimace in the face of the high gods, and at times a great contempt for the unkind masters of his destiny who ordained limitations for certain types of beings would find expression in horrid blasphemies, and doubts which should never have reached the final unpromising ecstasy of words. The sun streamed across the peaks of the mountains and flooded the valley with a yellow light that had a mist of dimness about the edges of it, and little white cottages, the handiwork of gnomes, stood out here and there between the boles of incredibly ancient oaks. Sandaris knew that beyond the mountains there was a sea and as he awoke with the damp smells of earth in his nostrils he fancied that he heard a great bell toll once solemnly far away in warning to some passing ship. Sandaris wondered whether the ship came from Carthage or Tyre, and if its captain wore a long beard and had cold green eyes.

Sandaris got quickly to his feet and flipped the dew from his small, furry ears. His teeth chattered in the still dawn, and his mythological lineage glittered in his moist, elfin eyes. He put a silver horn to his black lips and blew twice shrilly. When the Dryad came to him he reared himself abruptly on his stumpish, goatish legs and stared. The beauty of the Dryad cannot properly be described. Her eyes were as deep and hueful as the pale green water that decorous knights find in the moat of almost every Norman castle. Her lips never parted without saying that nothing else in the whole world mattered. Her breasts were voluptuously chaste, and a desire to possess them would have argued a courage and audacity hardly ever surpassed. Her thighs would have entranced Theocritus, and he would have invented a new language to praise them. She held out her arms to Sandaris and smiled.

"Sandaris," she said, "we are poor children crushed by the gods. Love me, dear. In my arms you will find revenge. We shall laugh at the gods. We shall go far away, you and I together, and I shall protect you from the might of high gods!"

Sandaris thought of the grail and its hard, pure and holy beauty. "Time does not corrupt it," thought Sandaris, "but the beauty of a woman is like an orchid that blooms once in the night and passes away forever." Sandaris did not know that the Dryad was skilled in magic and that it was her gift and privilege to read all thoughts.

"But you are also less than the leaf that falls and is trampled into the dust. And what does the grail avail when you are destined to an everlasting sleep? Will its cold beauty warm you, and fill your dead veins with desire? Is there pleasure in its frigid embrace? Would the grail kiss away your fears and give you a moment of ecstasy between two infinite voids? Think well, Sandaris. You will lie deeply in the earth and the years will pass over you, and you will never know again the sweet demands of youth. I am warm and soft, Sandaris. Yield, dear, to desire!"

Then Sandaris stepped quickly forward and took the Dryad into his arms. "She is more beautiful than the grail!" he said, and throwing back his head he laughed in the grace of God.

To Lewis Theobald Jun.

FROM A DEC. 1925 POSTCARD TO H. P. LOVECRAFT [PREVIOUSLY UNTITLED]

Hail Theobaldus, Prince of Singing Sires*
Whose Blakean vision thrives on Wrenish§ spires
Whose flaming genius soars from Pope to Poe
And on old Mather's pages, row on row
Descants, whose lucid wisdom shames the stars
Whose love of learning shakes our prison bars
And shows us worlds unknown, O Lewis Hail!
May every future quest attain the Grail!

Christmas
1925
F. B.

[The footnotes in this poem are Long's own. -PMG]

*Grandsires
§Christopher Wren, an obscure English architect (1632-1723)

POST CARD

THIS SIDE FOR CORRESPONDENCE

THE ADDRESS TO BE WRITTEN ON THIS SIDE

Hail Theobaldus, Prince of singing Sires*
Whose Blakean vision thrives on Wrenish* spires
Whose flaming genius soars from Pope to Poe
And o'er old Maturin's pages, row on row
Descants; Whose lucid wisdom shames the stars
Whose love of learning shakes our prison bars
And shows us worlds unknown, O Lewis Hail!
May every future quest attain the Grail!

Christmas 1925

F.B.

*Grandsire

*Christopher Wren, an obscure English architect (1632-1723)

H. P. Lovecraft
169 Clinton Street
Brooklyn
N. Y.

Lord Dunsany

FROM *L'ALOUETTE* (MARCH/APRIL 1926)

Liege-Lord of Elfin Wold, of Sunset Land
Beyond the fields and scarlet Earth we know,
Where proud, sea-faring Yann's dark waters flow
By Mandaroon, and star-girt Samarcand;
Where merchants spread athwart the yellow sand
Their flaming topazes, where griffins go
To lay their eggs, and where a crafty band
Of jolly seamen curse "poor Captain" so!

How near he seems to that rebellious king
Who sang of mountains cold against the dawn,
And one great sea that lay asleep in Spring
In Baiae's Bay on some bright careless morn:
How near he seems to Shelley, and how high
The quest which seeks a star in Beauty's sky!

Edward John Moreton Drax Plunkett, 18th Baron Dunsany
(1878 – 1957)

Don Adolphe Returns

FROM A LETTER TO H. P. LOVECRAFT DATED NOV. 2, 1928

Author of Monk[1] arrives in New York on S. S. Whydidn'titsink, and makes astounding assertion.

Declares Century Co. has *definitely* accepted Bierce book[2] for early spring publication

(and will set the type next week).

Young critic is skeptical, but interview with distinguished author fails to reveal trap.

Young critic is still looking for trap, however.

Young critic is firmly determined to refuse to undertake additional revision.

Don Adolphe[3] affirms that no new revision will be necessary and that Century Co.

is delighted with book in its present shape.

Don Adolphe merely wishes young critic to select a few passages for quotation from

Collected Works of Ambrose Bierce.

And young critic is still seeking trap.

Notes

[1]*The Monk and the Hangman's Daughter*

[2]*Portrait of Ambrose Bierce* by Adolphe de Castro (Century Company, 1929), which Long wrote a preface to.

[3]Long refers to Adolphe Danziger de Castro, who co-authored *The Monk and the Hangman's Daughter* with Ambrose Bierce and whom Lovecraft revised some tales for.

DON ADOLPHE RETURNS.

Author of Monk arrives in New York on S.S. Whydidn'titsink, and makes astounding assertion.

Declares Century Co. has definitely accepted Bierce book for early spring publication (and will set the type next week)

Young critic is skeptical, but interview with distinguished author fails to reveal trap.

Young critic is still looking for trap, however.

Young critic is firmly determined to refuse to undertake additional revision.

Don Adolphe affirms that no new revision will be necessary and that Century Co. is delighted with book in its present shape.

Don Adolphe merely wishes young critic to select a few passages for quotation from Collected Works of Ambrose Bierce.

And young critic is still seeking trap.

Ship Of Immortality - A Lament for Strange Tales

FROM A LETTER TO H. P. LOVECRAFT C. SEPT. 1933 [PREVIOUSLY UNTITLED]

I heard them calling in the streets
That the ship I serve upon—
The great ship immortality—
Was gone down, like the sun...

OCTOBER
STRANGE TALES
OF MYSTERY AND TERROR
25¢
A CLAYTON MAGAZINE
THE HUNTERS FROM BEYOND
By
CLARK ASHTON SMITH
And Others

Song of the Skymen

TAKEN FROM FBL'S STORY "THE SKY TRAP" FROM *COMET SCIENCE FICTION* (JULY 1941)

I'm a tough, true-hearted skyman,
Careless and all that, d'ye see
Never at fate a railer,
What is time or tide to me?
All must die when fate shall wit it,
I can never die but once,
I'm a tough, true-hearted skyman;
He who fears death is a dunce.

MAY 1941
20c
COMET
STF
STORIES OF SUPER TIME AND SPACE
Locked in Ice
Caverns on Neptune
in
ICE PLANET
by Carl Selwyn
— STF —
ERELICTS OF URANUS
by J. Harvey Haggard
— STF —
THE FACTS OF LIFE
by P. Schuyler Miller
— STF —
SKY TRAP
by Frank Belknap Long
— STF —
WE ARE ONE
by Eando Binder
— STF —
WHEN TIME ROLLED
BACK
by Ed Earl Repp
— STF —
EDITED BY
ORLIN TREMAINE

Venusian Folk Chant

From FBL's story "Shadow Over Venus"
From *Startling Stories* (March 1946)
[Previously Untitled]

From dawn to dusk
The Gule sits in its cage
Only the Gule
Which sits so quietly in its cage
Knows why the long grass withers
Only the Gule knows why sorrow dogs our footsteps
And destroys the work of our hands.

NOVEL OF THE FUTURE COMPLETE IN THIS ISSUE!
STARTLING
15¢
STORIES
MAR.
VALLEY OF THE Flame
A Novel of the Cat People
By KEITH HAMMOND
TWELVE HOURS TO LIVE
A Hall of Fame Classic
by CLARK ASHTON SMITH
A THRILLING PUBLICATION

Frank Belknap LONG

The Eye above the Mantel & Other Stories

THE EYE ABOVE THE MANTEL AND OTHER STORIES
Originally Published by Tsathoggua Press in 1995
Cover Illustration by Robert H. Knox

Introduction to THE EYE ABOVE THE MANTEL – Sire of Reanimator by Perry M. Grayson

Abbreviations:
EL: *The Early Long* (Doubleday, 1975)
LRS: H. P. Lovecraft. *Letters to Richard F. Searight* (Necronomicon Press, 1992)
SL: H. P. Lovecraft. *Selected Letters* (Arkham House, 1965-1976; 5 vols.)

Let's take a journey now through the corridors of space-time back to a simpler age. The year was 1920, and Frank Belknap Long was nineteen years old, living in New York. His interests were in literature, poetry, archaeology, and nature. Through a chain of unforeseen events, Long would abandon thoughts of becoming a naturalist and follow a path leading him 74 years into the future of a successful writing career.

The teenage FBL entered and won a writing contest in a juvenile magazine *The Boys' World*[1]. An award did not materialize in the shape of a plaque or trophy—but his work was published—and the most rewarding thing to come out of the event was Long's introduction to the world of amateur journalism. Shortly Frank Long was enlisted in the United Amateur Press Association, and he submitted a couple of short-short story manuscripts to the editor of the official organ, *The United Amateur*.

The first work to hit the 'ajay' scene from Long's pen was "Dr. Whitlock's Price" (*The United Amateur*, Mar. 1920) which was his credential[2]. "Dr. Whitlock" was followed a year later by the Poe-like phantasm "The Eye Above the Mantel" (*The United Amateur*, Mar. 1921). It was the latter that gained the interest of active UAPA member H.P. Lovecraft, who wrote Long a letter admiring the qualities of the story. That tale sparked a friendship and correspondence that would last nearly 16 years, until Lovecraft's death.

Long followed HPL into the pages of the small professional magazine *Home Brew*, which printed Lovecraft's "The Lurking Fear" and "Herbert West—Reanimator." Herbert West, HPL's medical student forever trying to bring life to dead tissue, is not far removed from Long's Dr. Whitlock, who had appeared only two years previously in *The United Amateur*. Both HPL & FBL had an affinity for Mary Wollstonecraft Shelley's *Frankenstein* motif, normally a grim subject. Long's cynical short story was definitely an influence on Lovecraft's "Herbert West" stories—which were written to order as a serial for *Home Brew*, a magazine that catered to the humorous. The West installments appeared under the heading "Grewsome Tales" and were not taken seriously by HPL at all. Lovecraft's love for making literary in-jokes and playful antics behind the scenes of ultimate cosmic horror began to manifest in a letter to Long dated Oct. 8, 1921, HPL wrote:

"I am calling the series *Herbert West—Reanimator*, since it deals with a young medical student with a penchant for revising the dead—a sort of advanced 'Dr. Whitlock', if I may allude to the work of a more distinguished author!" (SL I.158)

Further down the road the two literary men passed in-jokes back and forth. Long annihilated the character Howard (meant to be Howard Phillips Lovecraft) in FBL's July 1928 *Weird Tales* story "The Space-Eaters." And of course FBL elected to address the "forbidden" and non-existent Necronomicon in the opening of his "The Hounds of Tindalos," proclaiming John Dee (who Lovecraft said translated the fabricated Necronomicon into English) and Albert Einstein strange bedfellows (EL 50).

Later Long would borrow a few ideas from his friend, taking a bite out of HPL's famous Roman dream letter to include in "The Horror from the Hills," (*Weird Tales*, Jan. & Feb./Mar. 1931) and culling the "The Black Druid" (*Weird Tales*, July 1930) from a suggestion and unused plot germ of Lovecraft's.

An appendicitis called an abrupt halt to FBL's higher education at NYU in 1921, where he was majoring in journalism. On a whim, Long decided that he would pursue freelance writing. He realized that he had the knack for words, and felt he could make enough to survive as a freelance author. His thoughts on the subject weren't far off. It took a few years for FBL to both recover from his hospital stint and work himself into shape as a writer, during which time he wrote one more short-short for *The United Amateur*, together with several poems in prose and verse for *The United Amateur*, *Home Brew*, and other amateur journals and small magazines. Once HPL pushed him off to a start in the professional world, FBL didn't slow down for decades.

This volume collects all four of Frank Belknap Long's short-short stories (or vignettes) that appeared in amateur journals of the early 1920s and '30s, all of which display qualities that eventually made Long, alongside his friend Lovecraft, one of the most popularly reprinted authors in modern horror anthologies. Top editors such as Dashiell Hammett, Robert Arthur, Sam Moskowitz, August Derleth, Basil Davenport, Marvin Kaye, Leo Margulies, Robert Silverberg, Brian Aldiss, Tony Goodstone, and Ramsey Campbell to Stefan Dziemianowicz, Martin H. Greenberg, and Robert Weinberg have anthologized Long's stories. To date there are also five story collections under Frank Long's byline: *The Hounds of Tindalos* (1946)[3], *Odd Science Fiction* (1964), *The Rim of the Unknown* (1972), *Night Fear* (1979), and *Escape from Tomorrow* (1995). Without the stories herein, especially "The Eye Above the Mantel," Long might never have made Lovecraft's acquaintance and taken the steps to professional authorship.

"In the Tomb of Semenses" (Nov. 1921) was Long's last fictional piece in *The United Amateur*. Throughout the two years it took for Long to see professional publication he and Lovecraft were never far from one another —when HPL was in NY. The good literary friends visited the Poe cottage together with fellow amateur journalists James F. Morton and Paul Livingston Keil in 1922. By 1924 Lovecraft had succeeded in recommending his young friend's work to Edwin Baird, then editor of the new magazine *Weird Tales*.

In one last turn to amateur journalism, Long had a sardonic short entitled "A Dangerous Experiment" in *The Californian* in Fall 1934, several months before Robert H. Barlow published Long's second book of poetry. *The Goblin Tower* was a surprise gift from Barlow and Lovecraft, who helped set the type (LRS 69). "Sonny" Belknap, or Belknapius, as Lovecraft was wont to call him on occasion, was a mainstay of the NY Kalem Club and Lovecraft Circle. FBL often hosted meetings of the literary friends at the Long family apartment, with the hospitality of May Doty Long and Frank B. Long, Sr. (who had a home dentistry practice). Aside from his aunts, Barlow, and a few others, Long was the one person most frequently in HPL's company.

Come 1935 Long's writing career was off to a fast-paced start. With pseudo-scientific tales in *Astounding Stories* and two adventure yarns in *Oriental Stories* Long had succeeded as a freelancer much as he would continue to do for sixty years. The rest is history in the annals of fantastic literature. Five decades later Frank Belknap Long was acknowledged for his lifetime achievements as an author with the World Fantasy Award, the Gahan Wilson-designed bust of his comrade HPL. The connection between the two cosmic entities was strong, though Belknapius was the more romantic of the two. And the inspiration each author gained from the other ran deep through all Lovecraft and Long created. This collection will give the reader some insight into the early writings of the lesser known of the two weird literary men.

–Perry M. Grayson
West Hills, California
June 1995

Notes

[1]*The Boys' World* ran c. 1902-1935
[2]A work chosen to display an amateur journalist's skill to the veteran members of the amateur press association (APA).
[3]Reprinted with the exclusion of a few stories and with Long's introduction and notes for each tale as *The Early Long* (1975).

The Work of Frank Belknap Long, Jr. by H. P. Lovecraft

FROM *THE UNITED AMATEUR* (MAY 1924)

It is always a bit dangerous to hail an amateur spirit which seems to overtop the general level. That general level is so fastidiously jealous of its dignity, and so terribly quick to pounce on enthusiasts with its nasal accusations of ulterior motives and interested partiality! Wintry-blooded, elephant footed, the blind suspiciousness of literary senescence and stagnation will ever be with us to cry "puffing," quote old saws, and snickers out of court the subtleties it cannot understand. But because we have a civilised element equally permanent and even more deserving of attention, it will not do to let values perish altogether. That is why it is fitting at this juncture to call attention to a young writer who has brought us the first new touch of really creative vision we have had in years.

Frank Belknap Long, Jr., poet, critic, and weaver of fantastiques, is the writer in question. He stands above the crowd not because of any ultimate perfection of style or uniqueness of theme, for he is still youthful, changeful, and influenced by external models of varying laudability; but because of sheer daemonic ecstasy of creation and a passionate sensitiveness to the most delicate and imperceptible nuances of colour and beauty, which not more than one other amateur of today can be said to equal or surpass.

Mr. Long could not have risen to prominence at a more opportune time. With the fires of earlier literary revivals burning low, amateurdom is at present in the grip of a curiously stubborn devotion to outworn ideas and criteria. Generally speaking, we have lacked the vital modern element altogether; for even our ostensible rebels are definitely middle-aged and emotionally grounded in the past which they intellectually reject. It is not hard to define and explode this outworn tradition, for its characteristics are painfully clear. The tradition is one of tameness, imitativeness, and illusion—of exaggerated absorption in the meaningless routine of placid common life, unwarranted belief in vague relations between aesthetic pleasure and intellectual truth, and provincially disproportionate worship of clever littler writers like the Longfellow-Holmes clique, who merely conform agreeably to certain stilted backgrounds, affectations, and urbanities, without touching a single authentic emotion or possessing the least shade of truly original perception and insight.

Literary revolutions are not new. Elderly people who smirk complacently and predict the rapid subsidence of modernism forget utterly the Renaissance and even the romantic revival of the early nineteenth century. As in those times, the world has received a colossal influx of new ideas well calculated to remould all our impressions and recast all our utterances. We see the hollowness of things we believed before, and above all the disconnectedness of things we once thought indissolubly joined. It is the birth of new aesthetic, grounded on old but going beyond it, and demanding poignant, beautiful, and genuine sensation as the essence of artistic endeavour. Some of the old authors, of course, meet this demand; for the voice of unvarnished Nature never varies. But many fail to do so, because they wrote less from Nature than from false conceptions and interpretations of it, or merely copied those who went before. There is no literary value in a bleak transcript of others' feeling, convictions, and points of view. Paper is too expensive to waste on second-hand thoughts and images, however ambitiously served up. What we want are white-hot projections of individual personality, not cold grey reflections of the Babbit herd-psychology. Such projections Frank B. Long, almost alone among our newer amateur writers, succeeds in giving us.

The genius of Mr. Long is a spontaneous and self-expressive one. Educated in conventional American schools, and in New York and Columbia Universities[1], he has been thoroughly dosed with the traditional literature of the fathers; revolting only because he is too acute and aesthetically responsive to be satisfied with the obvious and platitudinous. Unaided he sensed the insincerity of the "museum hush" and the customary genuflection before dead and unmoving gods, and almost unguided he found his own voice among the light and colour and exotic beauty of the Italian Renaissance, the exquisite sensory adventuring of the French symbolists, and the delicate and polychrome dream-worlds that his ardent fancy bore of old legends, childhood moon-glimpses, and faintly reflected memories from far Mediterranean littoral where the water is deep blue and fragrant winds weave through broken marble colonnades on green seaward hills.

This may sound immature. Perhaps it would be if it were not to be considered as more than a starting-point. But a starting-point is precisely what it is, and its value lies in the perfect repudiation of the commonplace, and the adoption of free pagan beauty as a master, which it involves. For Mr. Long has passed the momentous barrier and learned the momentous lesson—that beauty is pleasure only, and to be taken joyously wherever found, irrespective of all antecedents and sequences. When he expresses himself it is purely to promote his personal aesthetic exaltation by means of beautiful, fantastic, or terrible arabesques, each independent, remote from prosaic life and associations, and conceived in a spirit essentially decorative; to satisfy with strange and emphatic imaginative symmetries a neural impulse both natural and insistent. And because that impulse is unmixed with love of fame, regard for convention, interest in the public, or any other vulgar ambition, but fulfilled in language of hauntingly original vitality and trippingly musical liquidity, Mr. Long is an artist.

II

The growth of Mr. Long's taste is keenly interesting to study. Appearing in amateurdom early in 1920 with a frankly boyish elementary story, "Dr. Whitlock's Price," his exceptional gifts were discerned by not more than one critic in all the associations. That critic, however, saw the single essential thing—that the young author's pictures were all authentic products of an actual visual imagination, and in no case blindly adapted from the lumber-room of previous juvenile reading. About this time Mr. Long wrote fiction voluminously, and with such meteorically rising power that his next published tale, "The Eye Above the Mantel," quite startled those who had judged its predecessor. It was in this tale that his intense originality, dramatic sense, and power of fantastic imagery first appeared to a marked degree. In November 1921, came "In the Tomb of Semenses," an Egyptian phantasy filled with musical and subtly rhythmical phrases, and opiate visions of "multi-coloured lights and the clanging-to of brazen portcullises," which proclaimed the genuine poet beneath a dress of prose. Subsequently Mr. Long, though not abandoning the field, wrote less fiction; as if realising that for the nonce his forte lay in the presentation of vivid, isolated, and luxurious pictures—single languorous impressions devoid of common thoughts and feelings, spiced with the riches of aloof introspection, and iridescent with extreme bizarrerie. For him was the heritage of Baudelaire.

Mr. Long as a prose-poet has evolved some unforgettable vignettes of grotesque-loveliness, alienage, and horror, and has attained heights which few amateurs share. Light, colour, sensation—all these essentials of pure art blend magically in such phantasms as "The Migration of Birds," "Flowers of Iniquity," "At the Home of Poe," "Unhappiness," or "Felis". "Felis" marked a new growth of Mr. Long's power, and although he has himself come to regard it as immature, its force and felicity are actually tremendous. There are one or two openings for illiterate snickers when it is read with uncomprehending verbal analysis, but what real critic can miss the sinister spell of the conclusion? . . . .

"Some day I shall drown in a sea of cats. I shall go down,
smothered by their embraces, feeling their warm breath
upon my face, gazing into their large eyes, hearing in my
ears their soft purring. I shall sink lazily down through
oceans of fur, between myriads of claws, clutching
innumerable tails, and I shall surrender my wretched soul

to the selfish and insatiable god of felines."

With this realisation of the artistic value of dissociated pictures and sensations, it is hardly singular that Mr. Long should turn to formal and rather Keatsian poetry. This he has done and is doing more and more; winning at least one prize and exciting considerable notice outside amateurdom, and being represented in our circle by such exquisite sonnets and lyrics as "The Inland Sea," "The Rebel,"[2] "Stallions of the Moon," and that inspired bit of elegiac pentameter called "Exotic Quest," which contains the vivid line, "Where golden griffins bathe in midnight meres." If this latter isolated specimen would seem to suggest precocity, a glimpse at the others quickly dispels that notion; for almost all the recent pieces bear evidences of Mr. Long's entrance into the mood of ironic modernism with its contempt for the grandiose and its sly juxtaposition of the mean and the fine, the commonplace and the exalted. Rhymed efforts in this vein have not been published in amateurdom, but we may grasp the mood equally well from the prose-poem "Ingenue," with its world-weary travesty on pedantry, loftiness, bombast, reverence, chivalry, connected ideas, and the trappings of tradition in general. Just what this ultra-modern saturninity will do to Mr. Long's naive creative energy we cannot say. The tendency in excess would be adverse, but it is probable that the artist's sheer emotional intensity will limit it in the end. For the moment it is perhaps useful in checking what might otherwise be an overdeveloped, ingenuousness or juvenile exuberance and extravagance.

It remains to consider Mr. Long as a critic, in which capacity he follows—as might be expected—the purely personal, subjective, and impressionistic methods of his favourite John Cowper Powys. He not to be overawed by the "scholastic-veneration-cult," nor is he ever afraid of enthusiasm. With his wide background and more than acute sensibilities he is among the very small group of amateurs really qualified to appraise fantastic and imaginative literature—perceiving points which the average calloused vision overlooks—and we may only hope that he will be given wide opportunities to aid in amateurdom's artistic revival. His few critical weaknesses are such as appear in dealing with cold-blooded analysis and the literature of philosophic intellection as distinguished from art. "An Amateur Humorist"[3] is the title of Mr. Long's best-known critique in our circle. This won Honourable Mention in the N.A.P.A. Essay Laureate contest in 1923.

As a whole, Mr. Long has in him something of the restless, questing aristocratic spirit of his beloved Italian Renaissance. His visual imagination is prodigious, and his taste for painting and sculpture exceptional. Only in aural imagination and musical appreciation does he feel limitations. He is a young faun strayed out of Arcady, innocent and vibrant, and eager to be himself sincerely in a world of mediocrity, repression, blindness, and stupidity. This is the assertive, unique personality which makes him a well-defined individual instead of a colourless rubber-stamp; which makes him a fearless pagan and a genuine artist. He is not yet mature—fine words and attitudes yet charm him a trifle more than they should, while his youthful ardour still leads him occasionally close to the borders of aesthetic dogmatism and unconscious humour—but he is rapidly maturing. With a finely strung organisation, limitless emotional force, and a mind wholly free from tawdry sentimentalised tastes and hampering false perspectives, Mr. Long has a future to which only a rash prophet would set limits. He is today the second-greatest creative artist remaining in amateur journalism.

Editor's Notes

[1]Long's appendicitis (c. 1921) called a halt to his less than 2 year college stay in the NYU School of Journalism. See *The Early Long*. Garden City, NY: Doubleday, 1975.

[2]*The United Amateur* 23, No. 1 (May 1924): 9. This is Long's first version of "The Rebel." A revised version was later printed in *In Mayan Splendor*. Sauk City, WI: Arkham House, 1977.

[3]*The Conservative* No. 12 (March 1923): 2-5.

HPL & FBL in New York circa 1931

Dr. Whitlock's Price

FROM *THE UNITED AMATEUR* (MARCH 1920)

"If it is successful," observed Whitlock, "we have made our name immortal."

The mellow light of an old-fashioned reading lamp threw into sight the faces of two men; the eyes of both glaring feverishly down at something which lay upon a large table.

The object moved, which satisfied the speaker.

"We have won," he said, in an even, unaffected tone. "Life has preserved"—and he turned on the electricity.

The room became instantly flooded with light and revealed the two men standing opposite each other; an excited expression on the face of one, while his companion bore a look of absolute calm.

Their hands were daubed with blood, which trickled off in little streams to the handsome blue velvet rug which covered the floor.

The room was large and comfortable. Rows of books lined the walls, and the aspect of the scene suggested the library of a successful man of affairs. Nothing could have been more out of place here than the large unpainted wooden table which stood in the middle of the room and which seemed to serve as a base for some sanguinary operation.

Both men were about forty, but in appearance their difference was radical and startling. One was a physical giant, with full and massive shoulders. It was he who had spoken, and who had remained calm throughout the operation. The other was a small, nervous man with a bristling moustache and rather long hair. He was irreproachably dressed, yet his white shirt-front was liberally bespattered with the crimson fluid just mentioned.

The object on the table suddenly became audible—it was an indescribable guttural sound or half-cry which proceeded from the pulsing throat.

The small man turned to the large one.

"Andrew," he murmured, "for God's sake, put an end to this thing. Our experiment is successful; far beyond out fondest hopes; but I can't beat to see that thing wriggle. It is hideous!"

"Bah, man!" returned Whitlock. "Your nerves are unstrung, that's all! What have we here? Just an ugly mass of protoplasm which I have managed to keep alive. A thousand such creatures sacrificed would be nothing. Brace up, Stephen; think of our glory—of the benefit to the race.

The creature, a large dog of mixed breed, was now groaning horribly. The poor thing was almost cut in two; and several of its most important organs had been removed. Its liver, still palpitating, lay alongside Whitlock's right hand. Suddenly its whole frame vibrated, and it died.

For the first time the large man let an exclamation of real feeling escape him. He uttered a slight groan. Then he turned to Stephen Gilbert.

"Doctor," he said, "the dog has died too soon. Our operation is not a success, but a failure. I must have another dog."

The one addressed turned and tried to argue.

"But Andrew," he protested, "you have had eight dogs already. I got this one only on condition that it would be the last; and now you ask for another."

"You will get me one and have it here by tomorrow," declared Whitlock, in a tone so decided that it was impossible to combat further.

Dr. Gilbert left the table without another word, disappeared for a few moments into another room, and returned with his hands washed and shirt changed. He then selected a cigar from the assortment on the table, took his cane, and left.

When the door had closed, Andrew Whitlock threw himself into a chair, and remained buried half the night in deep meditation.

When he had graduated from college he had possessed an independent income. It was small, but it enabled him to live without working; a state of affairs generally very bland, but occasionally very good for a young man.

In Whitlock's case it was advantageous. It had enabled him to build up his body instead of wearing it down by a high desk under a green lamp; so that at thirty he was a giant. Then he had resolved to embark upon something serious, so had undertaken the study of medicine.

At college he had met Stephen Gilbert, whose pupil he had become. Always brilliant, he had learned so rapidly that in the course of a few years he was clearly Gilbert's master.

It was then that he had conceived what he believed to be a revolution in surgery. The idea grew upon him and possessed him. He thought of it night and day. Then he confided his idea to Gilbert. At first the Doctor laughed; next he became serious; then he agreed to assist.

How short is the time between the conception of an idea and its application! We imagine something, and lo! we are doing it. We do not wait for the so-called psychological moment, but rashly make the plunge at once, whether for better or for worse.

Whitlock could not wait for anything. Wildly impatient to begin, he had a table erected in his library; and two nights after he had decided to make an experiment, the experiment was under way.

Within a week he had killed six dogs; or perhaps eight—since two more had perished from air-pressure in the box where it was necessary to keep them for two days before the operation. Yet in spite of the remonstrances of his friend he had continued. Now, on the threshold of success, he had failed at the last moment. But the passion had seized him. When would he stop?

The next day Gilbert brought Andrew Whitlock another dog, which was cordially welcomed. Whitlock was really enthusiastic. He was certain of success this time. The dog would not die, and they would be famous.

Gilbert, however, was more skeptical. He was humane, and objected to the extremes of vivisection. In spite of the obstinacy of Whitlock he tried to reason with him in every conceivable way, but he might better have argued with a rock.

Whitlock approached the table and beckoned for Gilbert to bring the small black-and-tan dog. Then, without the slightest show of mercy or relenting, he clutched the dog by the neck and fastened him down to the board. When everything was ready he turned to Dr. Gilbert.

"Now," he said in an even tone, "I am about to make one more attempt to regenerate dead cells. Are you ready?"

Gilbert nodded.

Whitlock's knife slowly descended. For one horrible moment there could be heard the sound of steel piercing flesh. Then all was over. The tenth dog was dead.

He turned to Gilbert. "You see," he said, "the dog was already sick." It died at the first thrust of the knife. I trust you will see that I get another."

Stephen Gilbert was exasperated beyond words. He talked, pleaded, remonstrated, and prayed Whitlock would give it up. The neighbors would hear the cries issuing from his house. He had no license. He would face a prison sentence.

But the friend only folded his arms and gave a cold, cynical laugh. It froze the bones and chilled the marrow. It forced a terrible thought to form itself in Gilbert's mind.

After all, was not Whitlock guilty of a horrible crime, even a series of crimes? What right had a man for his own personal ambition to torture dumb creatures? He resolved to take a stand in the matter.

"Andrew," he declared, "if you must continue with your experiments, we part company. I will no longer assist you." At first Whitlock seemed angered that his old friend should offer such a threat; then he controlled himself and spoke.

"Stephen, for eight years we have studied together. We have never differed in essential ideas. We have worked in harmony. Together we started out on this task. Are you going to fail me now?"

Dr. Gilbert was weak, and unable to maintain a stand even after he had taken it. The appeal of his friend moved him. After all, what was one more dog? So he gave his promise.

But one more sacrifice did not end the matter. On and on it went. Each time Gilbert would protest, but each time Andrew Whitlock would argue and win.

The winter passed and summer came. Twenty dumb creatures had paid the toll. It now became difficult for Whitlock to get rid of the bodies. The first three had been smuggled out of the house by Gilbert and thrown into the river with a stone tied to the bundle. But the river front was now carefully guarded, which made further disposition by this method impossible.

Whitlock thought of burning them, but as this would force the erection of a cremation furnace the idea was abandoned for the time being. Gilbert then resorted to the plan of carrying the dead things out into the country and throwing them into a lake.

Whitlock had become so absorbed in his pursuit that he neglected even his clothes. He seldom left the house, and when he did, it was only to secure some new surgical instrument.

One day he was exceedingly hilarious. He greeted Gilbert enthusiastically. He had discovered a new conglutinative agent. By applying this substance to open wounds, he could instantly stop all flow of blood without coagulation. Not only would his experiment be successful, but he would be able to make another one of even greater magnitude.

Gilbert was in despair. He was thoroughly tired of experimenting, but by this time he had learned the usefulness of his combating his friend's decisions.

Ten more canines perished, and Whitlock was still unsuccessful. Then the sluggish will of Stephen Gilbert asserted itself at last, and after a stormy scene he took the step he should have taken long before. Sadly he parted company with his friend forever, and Whitlock was forced to continue the work alone.

The summer passed, and winter was again approaching, yet still there was no advancement. What Whitlock was doing had now leaked out. Certain officials called upon him and demanded an explanation.

The "Society for the Prevention of Cruelty to Animals" sent a keen representative. But by the same force of character which had enabled him to win over Gilbert for such a length of time, he succeeded in convincing his accusers that there was nothing wrong.

On the tenth of November, Stephen Gilbert happened to pick up a certain medical paper. There in clear, black type, was the heading, "Unknown Experimenter Succeeds Where Others Failed," beneath which followed a brief account of how a certain Andrew Whitlock had created a new force in surgery by the regeneration of dead tissues.

By the twentieth every paper in the country was conspicuously printing the discovery. Whitlock was famous. If Gilbert remained at his post six months longer he would have shared the fame. But the doctor felt no remorse. Fame to him was a material thing; a disgrace to true merit. He was content to struggle along unknown if he could serve humanity.

Success went to Whitlock's head. Originally a cold man, obstinate and cruel, yet with a certain desire to help suffering humanity, he now became a libertine. He threw principle to the devil and spent his time in orgies. Excited beyond measure by his sudden reputation, and striving to forget the tortures he had inflicted upon nearly half a hundred dumb creatures, he ran the gamut of debauchery.

Three months after the announcement of his pupil's success, Gilbert noticed another item in the press; an item whose perusal caused him to turn pale. "I wonder what prompted Whitlock to take his own life?" he mused.

The Eye Above the Mantel

FROM *THE UNITED AMATEUR* (MARCH 1921)

I cannot recall to mind the precise place where we met, or even why we met. Perhaps we were assembled merely by chance, or perhaps we dared not consciously acknowledge the purpose which had brought us together. We had drunk a great deal of exceedingly rare and costly wine, and all sense of *proportion* had left us. We blasphemed openly, and uttered prophecies and warning which none but the gods have a right to utter. We also defied the little gods, and made fun of their tininess, which was unkind.

It seems to me that we were all very young, and students of a lore which has long since perished from the earth, even as the inspired and mystic writings of the Chaldees have sunk into oblivion with the forgotten centuries. I know that we interested ourselves in evolution, and speculated upon the creature which would someday take man's place upon this tiny planet of ours. That such a creature would come, we had not the slightest doubt, and we merely discussed the *way* of his coming.

But there was one among us who took no part in our conversation, but who sat with folded arms and smiling face, listening in silence to all which fell from our lips. He was tall and pale, and yet I cannot, I cannot for my life, describe him, or even hint at the unheard of characters which marked him as one apart, and which made us fear him with a fear which was more than human, a fear which the Sphinx must have felt when the gods of Egypt went shrieking across the Nile, to mingle with the gods of Greece and the gods of Rome. Of his dress,

I remember nothing save that the tails of his coat were immoderately long, and seemed to sweep the floor.

We feared him, and yet we dared not openly show our fear. Our gestures were violent and affected, and our voices low and constrained. And we looked at him constantly, and yet continued to talk of the superman. We continued to talk of the superman who would someday come and destroy the pallid and feeble thing called vir. And we thought of this superman as some great insect, with long hairy arms and loathsome, spider-like body, and we shuddered to think of that terrible day not far distant when the old lord of the earth should stand naked and defenseless before the new, and send up impotent shrieks to the quiet stars.

It was at this point that the stranger arose and laughed. I cannot think that such a laugh was known to the Egyptians, or to the Medes, or to the Persians, or to any of the lesser peoples who now dwell within the region of darkness. It was a laugh such as is only heard in the small hours of the night, when the gods are careless, and no longer watch over the meditations and manifestations of man. And the stranger spoke, and his voice was the voice of a daemon, but it was also the voice of an angel. And the stranger spoke, and his voice was unchaste, but it was holy. And I shuddered, and drew my coat up over my ears that I might not hear the voice that seemed to tempt me away from myself. And the others did likewise, but the voice reached us through our clothes.

"As the eye is the window of the soul, so is the eye of this room the window to that which is to come."

Upon hearing this we looked at one another, and our faces assumed expressions at once sinister and indescribable. There was but one window in that small room, and it was high up over a mantel of gold and onyx under a ceiling of white marble, and through it the pale light of the wan moon came in thin pencil-like rays.

In a moment we had placed a chair against the wall, a red-plush chair with arms of black ebony, and were mounting the mantel. But the mantel was narrow, and could not hold all of us, and seeing this, we became angry and fought among ourselves, and quarreled for a place on the mantel. And finally we decided to draw lots, and let fate decide who should be the first to mount, and to gaze through that little window which admitted the pale light of the wan moon in thin pencil-like rays.

And so one Amomenon produced a set of jet black dice, and for five minutes we gambled there under the little window to see who should be the first to mount. And, may the gods who watch over my destiny be praised, I *won*, and to me was reserved the privilege and the right of being the first, the first of all of the children of men, to look through that tiny window, and to view all that lay beyond.

And I mounted with glee, my heart beating within me, and my soul screaming with ecstasy. I mounted slowly, because the writings of Plith, the Babylonian, the ancient and yellow scrolls of Plith, had taught me that haste injures the bodily organs and destroys the faculties of the mind.

At length I reached the little window, and gazed out. I had expected to see a quiet Manhattan street, with yellow and black automobiles sweeping noiselessly by, and gentle lamp-posts shedding melancholy beams upon the well-turned mustaches of pale passers-by, and over all the wan moon which had shed its pale rays into the little room below though the tiny window at which I was now gazing.

But instead I beheld an endless waste stretching out for miles and miles, a quiet, empty waste of gray sandstone, utterly bereft of every living thing. The singing of birds, the drone of insects, and the sighing of the wind against the trees, and against the houses of brick and the palaces of marble—all had ceased, because there were no birds or insects or wind or palaces of marble and houses of brick.

For miles and miles the waste stretched out, and met the sky. And the sky was not blue, but yellow, and shed a yellow light over the gray sandstone. The sky itself shed this light, because there was no sun, or indication that there ever had been a sun. The light came from the sky, form every part of the sky, from out of infinite space came the light. And there were no birds or insects or wind or houses of brick and palaces of marble, but only the waste, endless, stretching away into infinity, crying out unto God.

And a hideous sense of foreboding hung over me, and I groaned inwardly, and was about to turn away from the window. But something arose in the distance—something white and terrible arose in the distance. From all sides it arose, they arose, myriad white things, and they came forward in even formation. They came forward from the place where the earth met the sky, and they marched with the sure and even step of an invading army.

And when they came near, and I beheld them, I screamed in dismay. For they were all white and tall, and were not like the men I knew. And then it dawned upon me with a fearful suddenness that these were not men at all, but were those of whom the Arabians wrote in letters of blood on secret tablets which have gone the way of all secret tablets.

And I stood with my eyes glued to the window, and watched them advance. I soon noticed that they were not all of the same size, and the tallest commanded the less tall. I also noticed that they wore no clothes but were covered with a kind of white fur, and that they were not ashamed of their nakedness. I also noticed that their teeth were black, and their eyes red and inflamed. And then they came very near, almost under the window, and I could hear them talk, and they spoke neither the tongue of Greece nor the tongue of Rome, neither the tongue of England nor the tongue of France, but held discourse in a strange tongue which I could not understand, and which I did not wish to understand.

And they kept coming and coming, and filled up the whole great expanse of gray sandstone, and became a titanic sea of ever-moving white.

And now they filled every square inch of all that land, and there was room for no more, and still some continued to come, crawling over the heads and shoulders of the others. And when at length they came no more, the yellow heavens went colourless, and the stars and the pale moon, which had shed its feeble mercuric light through the low window at which I now stood, became visible.

And then someone below spoke a command. It was uttered in a low voice, and it lacked authority, and yet I knew that it would be obeyed. I knew that the command would be obeyed, because it came from below.

And I was not mistaken, for lo, as I stood there, a path was cleared among the multitude of white beings who swayed to and fro under the colourless sky, and the pale moon, and the quiet stars.

And the path was a shocking path, very narrow and uneven, and ever in danger of being closed up by the angry white things that had made it. And the path extended from the window to the place where the earth met the sky. And I kept my face pressed to the window, watching the path.

Of a sudden there arose on the horizon four white figures, but taller than any that had gone before, as tall as the Arabian goddess Aso who rules over the hearts of all brave men. And these four figures came forward, and they carried with them a great thing of bronze and of iron, a great heavy thing of bronze and iron that resembled nothing so much as a cage.

And when they came very near I saw that it *was* a cage, and I cried out to the gods of Seth and Sarmenia to take forever from me my sight, that I might not behold the thing within that cage. For the thing within that cage was hideous to look upon, and was covered with foul yellow mud and dank Charonian vegetation, and it uttered little feeble cries which reminded me of the cries which Heth had uttered when he had been attacked by the lampreys in his master's garden, and had suffered his blood to be drawn off in eighteen different directions at the same time.

But the gods of Seth and Sarmenia heard me not, and my sight never left me, and I was forced to keep my eyes riveted upon the cage of iron and bronze and the loathsome thing within. And while I watched, the white creatures began to torture their captive with little sticks of wood, little sharp sticks they which they held in their hands. they poked him in the face, and hit him over the head and shoulders, and called him names which I knew were shocking because of the voice in which they were uttered. But, strange to say, I felt sympathy only for myself, because the creature was too horrid to excite sympathy in either man or beast. And the moon and the stars looked down silently, and said nothing, and the cries of the thing went up to the colourless heavens with no one to protest.

How long I continued to watch them torture the thing, I cannot tell, but it seems to me that for ages and ages, aeons and aeons, the cries rose up to the gods. And at length the light of the moon fell full upon the cage, and the thing within stood out in awful clearness.

And now as I write, my soul becomes delirious, and my heart volcanic, and my mind alone remains calm. for the thing within that cage—I am all consumed with fire—I cannot write it—I cannot—this wretched soul—but enough—I will tell all—the thing within that cage was a man, and that man was *Kunos*, my dear, my darling brother! O God, the loathsome thing within covered with dark Charonian vegetation was flesh of my flesh, and bone of my bone!

I tried to turn from the window—I sent up supplications to both the little gods and the big gods; and I even invoked the aid of the sinister and unchaste daemon Roth who dwells within the vile Dagaan charnel house, and who is part ruler of Eld and Nomore. But my prayers were unanswered, and to me of all men was reserved the horrible fate of being forced to gaze upon the living disintegration of a loved one.

And when at length it was over, and dear Kunos had gone his way into the endless void, the gods of Seth and Sarmenia, and of Rosath and Raynald, gave permission to leave the window. And, with a shriek which I did not recognise as my own, I jumped down from the mantel, and screamed to my companions to cover me with their cloaks, and to shield me from myself. But my companions heard me not, for my companions, alas, were beyond hearing and seeing! My companions were beyond hearing and seeing, and they neither heard my cries, nor noticed the agony of my soul.

Stretched out pale and motionless they lay in a neat row upon the cold floor of white marble—stretched out stiff and silent they lay.

And upon the lips of each there was a smile, and upon the breast of each a little red spot—a little, neat, round red spot upon the breast of each. And then with a fearful suddenness it all came to me, and I knew that the Egyptians, and the Medes, and the Assyrians and the Persians were all more cunning than we—all infinitely more cunning than we—because *they* had *known*, and had permitted their civilisations to sink into decay, and had left to the Celt and the Saxon the terrible menace of the superman.

And now I saw him standing there, the new lord of the universe, standing there, standing there quiet and sinister over the bodies of those whom he had slain. And then he suddenly seemed to perceive that I was no longer at the window, and he smiled with sweet smile, and spoke in a voice which was tender and soft.

"You are the last of your kind, and I pity you. Go, and live to revel in the glories of a civilisation which is to come, a civilisation such as you have never known. Go, I say, and wander among the graves of your race, and if you so desire, write the history of my coming!"

And I obeyed.

In the Tomb of Semenses

FROM *THE UNITED AMATEUR* (NOVEMBER 1921)

Strange indeed are the ways of the ancient gods! To me, a humble scribe, and a lowly dreamer of dreams, they have granted an understanding of those melancholy signs and portents which foretell the end. Thus I know that even as I write this, the mantle of Osiris descends upon the world. For now all of those marvelous things prophesied in the yellow scrolls of Amenses, which lie buried at Thebes near the catacombs of the Pharaohs, have come to pass, and the moon is the colour of blood, and the scintillating pole-star retreats shrieking into the infinite blackness beyond the multi-hued suns.

In the solemn gray cities of the West, in the charcoal-burning cities of the West, men walk the streets with slow and muffled steps, and with an incubus of silence upon their souls. And in the great white castles by the sea, kings and emperors sit among their handmaids, and attired in spotless robes sip costly green wine from cups of alabaster, and seek forgetfulness in revelry and sin. But some at least are wise, and know that the end is near, that the sun is burning less brightly, and that a frightful cold creeps rapidly equatorward from the purple poles. Even now all of the soft, sweet, gentle noises and little sounds of this workday have ceased, and there remain only the ominous croaking of frogs on the edges of dank, brackish tarns, and the shocking laughter of the mad in the streets of London. Because of these things, I write boldly knowing full well that what I here inscribe with a quill pen on a sheet of faded papyrus shall never be read by any mortal man.

I cannot remember when it was that I went into the land of yellow spectres to study the mummies in the catacombs of the Pharaohs. I know that it was many years after the last of the great plagues, and that many strange things had come about among the living. I remember that gods in the form of men built great engines of brass and of iron which ploughed their way over the land, and great ships of wood, and of steel, and even of stone, which carried thousands of their kind over the ocean, over that terrible and endless sea whose immensity had paralysed the faculties of Setses, the greatest of the unremembered Pharaohs.

I had a purpose in going into Egypt, and I talked vaguely of Archaeology of excavations, and of the Royal Society, but in truth I cared not for these things, but only for the visions which the dead evoked, only for the heathenish and unhallowed vision which the finely-wound mummies evoked. For days and days I had wandered over the yellow sand, within the shadows of the Pyramids, dreaming the dreams of unremembered kings, and absorbing into my very being all of the solemn melancholy of a stately and glorious past. For days and days I had sat among the reliquaries of well-ordered civilisations which had flourished on the banks of the Nile when my ancestors were wretched ape-men crawling through the rifts of Java, civilisations which were no more when the first sun-baked bricks of unhappy Babylon were laid by a Semitic prince.

And then one night when the Egyptian moon seemed more menacing than usual, a daemon took possession of me and bade me do a terrible deed. I was to creep stealthily into the tomb of Semenses, into the awful sepulchre of the great and mighty king who ruled over the children of Ammon in the lonesome years before the gods were created, and with a knife of gold I was to sever from the body the head of the most venerable of Pharaohs. For Semenses lies stretched at full length upon a marble slab, and although he is enshrouded in seven cerements his head remains uncovered in the darkness.

I listened to the holy scribes and eunuchs of Thebes discuss in awed whispers the glories of the sacred sepulchre, and heard them tell how five and twenty wives sit nightly by the side of the royal corpse, and stroke its long white hair, and whisper sweet secrets into its ear, and comfort it with their kisses. Of course I laughed at these things, seeing no reason why five and twenty wives should thus humour a mummy whose days of greatness were past. But when the holy scribes and eunuchs saw me blaspheming, they crossed themselves and bade me be gone, and one even threatened me with his staff of ebony. With a shocking laugh, I left them, and prepared to enter the house of the dead.

I first anointed myself with oil, that the spells of the succubi and vampires which haunt the deceased might not avail against me. Then I clothed myself in raiment befitting my station, and selected a staff of ivory with which to defend myself against the attacks of bats, whose duty it is to destroy all those who approach the Pharaohs. I also placed upon the third finger of my left hand the ring which I had received from Queen Asamia in my fifth incarnation, and which I had found again in my twentieth. Thus fully prepared to defy every Egyptian god, I left Thebes, and journeyed toward the tomb of Semenses the Great, wearer of the double crown, and favoured of Ammon and Month.

The tomb of Semenses is of reddish stone, and rises obliquely from out of the sands. No one knows by whom it was built, or even why it was built. Perhaps it was once a charnel house, or perhaps the lesser gods assembled there to pray to the greater gods. It was never meant to hide the bones of a king, and the scribes and eunuchs say that the *ka* of the dead Pharaoh was furious when it found itself entombed in so unchaste a place. Indeed, its wrath was terrible to behold, and eight of the five and twenty wives fainted, and six sought refuge behind the marble slab.

The moon was high in the heavens when I reached the sinister vault. I carried a torch, that I might gaze well upon the features of the dead king, and in my belt was the knife of gold with which I was to do my loathsome deed. I approached cautiously from out of the semi-darkness and laid my hand nervously upon the ancient bolt which fastened the great stone door. Silently I removed it, and, my heart beating wildly within me, I entered the hallowed tomb.

Within there was a great darkness, and my torch shed but a feeble light. But by its dim rays I could distinguish long rows of fatuous

Sphinxes, and the sacred marbles, and a loathsome effigy of an alien god with a face so hideous I cannot describe it, and the charming altars which were erected there to all of the kind little local gods—to Eras and Hos and Sesbet. And I also saw altars dedicated to Month and Miu and Nechbet and Nieth. And I saw tablets of bronze on which were inscribed the names of great gods, even Ammon and Isis and Hathor and Man and Osiris and Set. I could discern in the darkness the trays of gold bearing the *ka's* food, which consisted of lampreys steeped in oil; and the robes of red velvet lined with ermine, which the dead monarch's double donned upon occasion. But search as I might, I could find no traces of Semenses, neither could I hear the sweet-toned voices of his five and twenty wives.

And then as I stood there meditating upon my failure to discover the secrets of the most ancient of kings, the bats attacked me. They came out from behind the sacred marbles, and fell upon me from above. They were as large as Egyptian lions, and they fought like the ancestral cats of Hathor. They were large and brown, with opaque wings, and they fought like daemons. And they sunk their black teeth into my arms and legs, and although I struck at them madly with my staff of Persian ivory, they refused to be driven off. And then I thought of all of the evil spells which Arabes my tutor had taught me when I was a golden-haired page in my father's castle, and I used them against the bats; but the creatures of darkness were not destroyed, and they buried their fangs yet deeper into my members. And then I called upon Yahwe, the god of the Jews to deliver me from my unmerciful enemies, and Yahwe heard my prayers. The god of the Israelites heard my prayers, and he had begun to shake the sepulchre in his mighty wrath when the bats withdrew of their own accord and retreated snarling behind the bronze dedicated to Ammon. Now to this day I do not know whether the bats feared Yahwe, or whether the strange creatures admired my courage, and desired not to destroy a brave man. But I was nonetheless grateful for my miraculous deliverance, and falling upon my knees, I gave thanks to this jealous alien god of an exotic race. And I have since held Yahwe in the greatest respect, although I worship other gods.

And then as I knelt upon the damp floor of that antique sepulchre, a strange and wondrous thing happened. The stones and effigies about me became luminous, and glowed with a soft silvery light, and a fiery square formed upon the wall in back of the row of fatuous Sphinxes. In astonishment and fear, I arose to my feet, only to see the marble slab bearing the body of Semenses come slowly toward me from out of the flaming square.

With a shriek I retreated until my back was against the opposite wall. There I sought to defend myself against the advancing bier by chanting old hymns stolen from mystic papyri of the greatest of the sun-prophets, Cyran Sasania, and by intoning the syllables of the funeral ode which Phar Monsemenses had composed over the body of my benefactress and queen, the Princess Asamia. But the louder I chanted the swifter the slab advanced, and I saw with horror that if I acted not, I should be crushed into shapeless pulp against the dark wall of the terrible vault.

For a moment I hesitated, and then muttering a prayer which I had learned from Arabes, I drew the golden knife from my belt and hurled it at the hoary head of the ancient monarch. I cannot remember what happened after that, but it seems to me that I very nearly entered into the bosom of Osiris. I have memories of multi-colored light and the clanging to of brazen portcullises, and of sweet whispering and gentle sighs which seem to belong to this period. Certainly I was lifted up and carried a great distance, and certainly aeons and aoens elapsed ere I recovered consciousness. When I finally awoke, it was to find myself in the open desert under the hot tropical sun, gazing up into the face of one whom I shall not describe, because I cannot.

Never in all my dreams have I ever thought that there could be such a woman. I have said that I cannot describe her, and yet I can hint at the characters which made her more to me than all of the gold in treasuries of the charcoal-burning cities of the West, more than all of the priceless hoards in the solemn black cities of the West. Her hair was as yellow as the Egyptian sands, and it glowed like burnished gold; her forehead was high and majestic as the forehead of the Princess Asamia; her eyes were blue and liquescent as the enchanted fish-pools of Eldenheim, and they sparked with the brilliancy of the diamond; her nose was of Grecian mold with all of the haughtiness of the Roman; her lips were as full and rosy as the lips of the noble Hypatia; her teeth were as white, as smooth and as even as the sacred marbles; and her laugh was as silvery and melodious as the pagan piping of the great Pan. But from the first it was not love which drew me toward this strange nymph of the desert. Rather was it the exaltation of the soul which I felt when gazing upon her unrivalled beauty. When I looked into her eyes, I seemed to see Rome at the height of her splendour and power. When I gazed upon her nose, I saw revealed the silent glories of Greece at her intellectual zenith. When I beheld her lips, it was as if I were beholding all of the solemn splendours of the Renaissance, all of the romance of Europe. And when I looked upon her forehead, I saw all of the teeming millions in the charcoal-burning cities of the West. In her I beheld the beginning and the end, the past and the present, the new and the old. She was life incarnate, and she represented all of the achievements of man.

As I lay in the yellow sands watching with ecstasy her every movement, she stroked my hair, which had grown to a fabulous length, and told me that she was the favourite wife of Semenses, and that her name was Raidee, and that she had saved me from the wrath of the local gods. The mighty gods had not been vexed by my deed, because they were jealous of Semenses and desired to see him humbled.

Would that I could banish from my consciousness all else but the memories of the days that I spent at the feet of Raidee. Would that I could forget all else but the visions of the magic hours I spent at the feet of the wife of Semenses. My days among the living are few, but not for the promise of eternal life would I sacrifice one of those glorious images of other times and places. To know the secrets of aeons long vanished, to behold the magic of the Chaldees and the wizardry of the Medes, to listen to words of wisdom from the lips of gentle seers long since dead, to sit cross-legged before the wonder-fires of the Persians, and to chant tribal lays forgotten in the dim vistas of yesteryear, to explore the heavens with the tiny bearded astrologers of Sera, and to trace the courses of stars which have become weary of burning and which have left the known universe to wander aimlessly through the aetherless infinity beyond the red and yellow suns, to call up the memories of a thousand vanished scenes of royal splendour and unrivalled pomp—ah, Raidee, Raidee, must I forever lose you? Must I forever forego these pleasures of a poet's soul?

It was on the seventh night after my entry into the tomb of Semenses that the thing happened. I thought that I loved the beautiful Raidee. Mad that I was—I fancied—I fancied that it was not the dreams which her beauty evoked which enchanted me, but rather was it the love of man for woman. I imagined that it was not exaltation of the soul but exaltation of the heart which I felt at the sight of this wondrous creature. And so when the moon was high in the heavens, and when the Sphinx had nodded and fallen into deep slumber, I arose from the yellow sands, and took in my arms the wife of Semenses.

I arose from the yellow sands, and clasped to my bosom the gentle Raidee, and then—and then I drew back trembling and shuddering and aghast, for the thing within my arms—can I ever bring myself to write it?—the thing within my arms was a withered mummy, and upon its shrunken breast was the mark of the First Dynasty, and upon its forehead the sacred seal of Semenses! Yes, the thing within my arms was an ancient corpse preserved with spice and wound with a pale green cerecloth, and upon its antique breast there were the mysterious markings of the First Dynasty, and upon its forehead the unholy signature of the most ancient of kings. O Ammon, I have suffered much, but the memory of this affliction has withered my soul, and I shall never dream again.

I left Egypt, and returned to the solemn black cities of the West. I am glad that the end is near, that the sun is burning less brightly, and that a frightful cold creeps rapidly equatorward from the purple poles. Anon I am glad that the scintillating polestar retreats shrieking into the infinite blackness beyond the multi-hued suns, because I long to enter into the bosom of Osiris. I long to enter into the bosom of Osiris, and to forget.

A Dangerous Experiment

FROM *THE CALIFORNIAN* (FALL 1934)

A number of years ago I spent nearly sixteen months in the East Indies. I visited Java and the Straits Settlements, and was a guest for several weeks of a business associate in Singapore. My friend's home was in the suburbs, entirely removed from the exotic world of color and glamor through which I had been traveling. He was an Englishman, and everything about the place was English. On the complexion of the servants dispelled the illusion which these circumstances would otherwise have produced—the illusion that I had passed overnight from the confusion and babel of the Orient to an English country estate. My friend had four servants. Three of them were Chinamen, and one was a Malay. The Malay spoke excellent English, and seemed an extraordinarily intelligent person in all respects.

One night when my friend and his wife and two elderly neighbors were sitting on the veranda I encountered the Malay in the garden. There was a garden-seat near at hand, and I motioned him to sit down, giving him to understand that I wanted to talk to him.

He sat down, dutifully enough. And then I asked him a question that had been on the tip of my tongue for some time. I asked him why Malays ran amuck. It was a simple enough question, and I think he understood why I wanted to know. In all my experience during nearly two years of travel, I had never seen a Malay run amuck, and I wasn't at all certain that the impulse was natural and instinctive as the writers of travel-books liked to pretend. I wanted to find out.

"Is it part of your religion?" I asked him. "Are you taught that it is good—right? Are you taught that? Or is it something that can't be helped, that just comes, like a sickness?"

He looked at me for a moment in silence. "It might happen to anyone," he said, suddenly. "It might happen at any time."

"It comes from within then?" I persisted. "It's a natural urge, a sudden overpowering impulse? You're not taught that it's the right thing to do?"

He shook his head. "We're taught," he said. "But it comes all the same. Even without the teaching it would come. There is nothing could stop it. It might happen to anyone. *It might happen to me.*"

I was startled. I looked at him in sudden alarm. He was staring past me, at the ladies on the veranda. A strange glow had crept into his eyes.

The idea was preposterous, and yet—I had heard that it required very little to set a Malay off. A suggestion, a careless hint, was sufficient. I had laughed at such stories, but what if they were really true.

And then, like a flash, it *seemed* to happen. I saw the Malay's hand fly to his belt and the knife come out. I saw him leap forward toward the people on the porch. I heard their screams. It was horrible, sickening. I heard my friend cry out, saw him throw his arms before his face in a frantic, futile effort to save himself. I saw him fall. I saw his wife fall, stabbed to the heart. I saw the two old ladies go down, clutching frantically at the mosquito-screens with gnarled hands, in an extremity of agony and horror, dragging the screens with them as they collapsed in a heap at the Malay's feet.

In a moment it was over, and the Malay was running shrieking through the garden, an encrimsoned maniac. The blood lust, the lust to kill and maim, was clear upon him.

Slowly the vision dissolved. The Malay was sitting quietly beside me, nodding to himself. The glow had gone out of his eyes. Or perhaps I had merely imagined it. Perhaps there had been no glow at all. My relief was so great that I nearly fainted.

"We cannot resist when it comes," said the Malay, rising. "But it very seldom happens. Only when a man has been ill, when he has been ill a long while. Something happens to him then. He can't help it, it is not his fault, but he feels all shut in. He must run amuck or go mad."

He left me then, nodding reassuringly. For a moment I sat without moving. Then I got up and walked to the veranda. The old ladies nodded affably, but I said nothing. I merely sat down, removed my hat, and helped myself to a whiskey and soda. "They do not suspect," I thought, "That I have been tempting fate." I wiped the sweat from my forehead, and tried to speak casually to the old ladies, and my friend's wife. But I couldn't. My tongue adhered to the roof of my mouth, and I was short of breath, and my heart was pounding tumultuously. To this day I still often wonder what they thought of my strange behavior.

An Epistle to Francis, Lord Belknap by H. P. Lovecraft

TO A SOPHISTICATED YOUNG GENTLEMAN PRESENTED BY HIS GRANDFATHER WITH A VOLUME OF CONTEMPORARY LITERATURE - CHRISTMAS 1928

Ingenious Age once more essays to find
A proper gift for youth's sophistick mind,
Well tho' he know how bootless 'tis to send
Aught that his old head can comprehend
Preplext, the Grandsire scours the stalls to chuse
Some spawn of Chaos and the bedlam Muse;
Some complex fruit of multiple dimension,
With modern outlines and remote pretensions,
Which, scorning Euclid and the pedant race,
Revots from Time, and flings a sneer at Space;
Of wit and beauty keeps discreetly chary,
And forgets sense to be contemporary.
What can best suit so deep a disillusion,
And cater to such civilis'd confusion?
Whose pen indeed the wrought-steel crown deserves
As Cham of cubes, and Arbiter of curves?
For sure, 'twere vain on normal art to lean
In youth's jazz'd world of concrete and machine!

Gods of the Waste Land! say what monster new
Shou'd grace a shelf by *Benda* or *Luleu*?
What best befits a bookcase carv'd to ape
An airplane's angles or a subway's shape?
Subtle the style that fits our motor nation,
Smooth as a *Ford*, prim as a filling-station,
Mass'd and severe as yonder office tow'r,
Short in its wave-length, statick in its pow'r;
High as the crown of *Mencken's* scornful hat,
Objective as a *Times-Square* Automat;
Devoid of pomp as *Woolworth's* or *McCrory's*,
And cerebral as *Vogue* or *Snappy Stories;*
Mature as moonshine booze, and free of bunk
As the frank perfume of the candid skunk;
Gay as a billboard, ardent as the graphick
And muddled as a stream of Broadway traffick;
Firm as a gangster or a stick-up man,
Ironick as an old tomato-can,
As radio loud, as movies democratick,
Symolick as a Greenwich Village attick;
Bright as the tungsten of a *Wrigley* "ad,"
And settled as the latest sideburn fad—
Thus the deep lines that may alone express
Our whirling epoch in its rightful dress!
But who, mid our embarrassment of riches,
Wears the true laureate's four-plus flannel breeches?
See in what throngs th' ambitious candidate
Crashes and storms—and sometimes gets—the gate!
Here *Joyce* appears with Odysseys demure,
His prose a junk-pile, and his mind a sewer;
Hard on the heels the *Hechtick* hero hurtles,
With rose-tipt beak, and twin'd with Paphian myrtles.
Wise *Eliot* stalks in state—no friend of cant he—
And stores a cosmos in a triple "Shantih";

Cursing all caps, the comely *Cummings* comes,
And *Lindsay* pounds his syncopated drums;
With fun and folklore struts romantick *Cabell*,
Chalking his half-hid smut behind the stable;
Stein formless foams, and chants the tender button,
Whilst *Arlen's* wisecracks knowing saps may glut on.
Cubist and futurist combine to shew
Sublimer heights in *Kreymborg* and *Cocteau;*
The shade of *Huysmans* reddens prose and rhyme,
And fiction soars in *Burke* and *Bodenheim*.
Assist, ye brazen Nymphs of *Montparnassus,*
To chuse a chief from the bold hordes that gas us:
Say what pied knight of these assorted lots
Outshines with broken lines or rows of dots?
Tell aged Ignorance what seer to pick
As symbol of a world gone lunatick.
Count them all o'er, and find a name to lead
A dizzy universe of nameless speed.
How shall we do it? Simple as the day!—
Listen intent whilst modern criticks bray.
Weigh the wild clamour, and proclaim as proudest
The jumbled scribe whose name is heard the loudest.
Him we elect, and to the heights promote
As King Sophisticate by true straw vote.
His words alone we hold supremely fit
To feast a flaming youth of modern wit.
Hark! One—two—three!—the long-ear'd herd decide
On a vague ghost to their aesthete-guide:
Hail to the chief their phrensy'd pladits boost—
And take, Young Man, a tome by MARCEL PROUST!

HPL & FBL in New York circa 1931

Four poems to FBL by H. P. Lovecraft

I

Whilst you invade with prattling joy
The chrome-blue swamp oneiroscopick,
And like a multivalent boy
Divagate some bidextrous topick;
Whilst, as I say, you thus amuse
A modern world with Eliot leanings,
Pray laugh not if your Grandpa choose
A simpler rhyme, and one with meanings.
We old folks know, of course, the world
Is but a chaos frail and vicious;
A very rubbish-vortex, hurl'd
In shapes delusive and capricious;
But split me, Child, if we can men
Our stale empirick imperfection,
Or keep from making outlines blend
The way they do before dissection!
And so tonight with pen in hand
Two wish the blessings of the season,
I'm curst if I can well command
The mode in analytick reason!
I can't take Santa Claus apart,
In shreds denigrate with strabismus,

So, Child, I'll quit the quest of art,
And wish an Old Man's Merry Christmas!

II

As ev'ry year the Farmer's Almanack
Tell us that Christmas once again is back,
Our thoughts ancestral turn to former days,
And old dreams flick o'er the fagot's blaze.
Take, then, this token, by a patriarch penn'd,
Who would to youth the antient lore commend,
Nor scorn that art which elder souls admire,
Flung whitely heav'nward in a Georgian spire!

III

At thee, decadent Sir, this tome is hurl'd,
Appropriate to a purple-incense world;
O'er each strange leaf with Mediterranean zeal
The dodd'ring donor bids thy vision steal:
'Tis Greek to him—the simple country squire—
But youth is youth, and age respects its fire!

IV

A plain old soul, nor sharp nor analytical,
Seeks here in all sincerity to please
A modern Child, sophisticate and critical,
Who finds our world a wearisome disease.
Take this volume, lofty and fastidious,
Where disillusion shakes its scornful head;
Ne'er will the donor frown with glance insidious,
Tho' deep thou study what he hath not read!

At the Haunt of a Cosmic Entity by Perry M. Grayson

IN MEMORY OF FRANK BELKNAP LONG, JR. (1901-1994)

Kneeling by this sepulcher of the dark,
Joined by autumn gusts and skeleton oaks,
In the eternal quest for the crimson stars,
And thirst to hear calls of kindred folks,
Whose imaginations knew no boundaries,
But plumbed the breadth of dimensional space,
Recording ethereal tragedies,
Fantastic terrors of alien face.

Open myself up to the graying sky,
Twilight sun and the space-borne blend,
Tracing constellations through their minds,
Gone beyond the summits of human ken,
With romance of knowledge and Earth,
And cosmic emotions streaming forth,
The sum struggle of a galactic race—
Sorcerous words that assailed icy waste

-Perry M. Grayson
3 November 1994
Brighton Beach, Brooklyn, New York

THE GOBLIN TOWER Reviewed by Ernest A. Edkins

FROM *CAUSERIE* (FEB. 1936)

When the versatile editor of *The Dragon Fly* decided to tackle bookbinding, he assembled a group of Frank Long's early poems for his venture. The intent was to surprise Mr. Long, who was not only surprised, but possibly taken somewhat aback. Otherwise, he might have been disposed to remonstrate over the inclusion of verses that obviously were written during the uncritical ardor of adolescence. But, as Mr. Barlow[1] explained to me in a recent note, these immature poems are certainly no worse—if, indeed, they are decidedly better—than the *juvenilia* of Keats; a connotation which I hope will serve to assuage Mr. Long's embarrassment.

The Goblin Tower [2], printed on a small press under discouraging conditions and bound with equally primitive equipment, does vast credit to its publisher. It is really a fine first attempt, and my heart warms to the lad who was able to accomplish so much, with so little. The booklet is backed with a deep rose buckram (or some such material) and boarded in an antique ivory tone—a most attractive color scheme. The title page is tastefully executed in black and red, and the edition is limited to 100 copies, at $1.00 each. If there are any sportsmen in amateur journalism they will send in their subscriptions promptly, thus encouraging the

Dragon Fly Press to produce other books. Mr. Barlow had displayed courage and initiative; he should not be left holding the bag.

To review this collection of poems is a delicate task. Mr. Long cannot be blamed for the resurrection of his early indiscretions, and Mr. Barlow certainly deserves praise for his enterprise, if not his selection. Yet due notice must be taken of this book, which is an important event in amateur literature, and of the verses, which disclose the well-springs of Mr. Long's subsequent work as a talented writer in the field of prose phantasy.

With some notable exceptions these poems are written in what might be termed the "weird" *genre*. They describe fantastic landscapes, fabulous monsters, gruesome dreams. Every line is designed to evoke a shudder, every image a Shape of Fear. In the legendary habitat of "Great Chaugnar"[3]

"A billion miles beyond the suns,"

a "mindless hate" meditates the annihilation of our doomed planet, whereupon the poet hopes to avert this calamity by genuflections. On "Icy Kinarth"[4] he dreams amidst prehistoric reptiles, while at the base of that frozen crag black waves cleverly contrive to lap "the Isle of Spice." Elsewhere, Medusa's head is inconsiderately exhumed by a morbid individual who delves in the "Horror on Dagoth Wold,"[5] and in some other macabre lines attributed to "An Old Wife,"[6] the nocturnal orgies of Succubi, witches, devils, and "the godless dead" are recited with hellish gusto.

Mr. Long, for whose brilliant abilities I have the greatest admiration, will, I am sure, forgive me for saying that these *diableries* leave me somewhat cold. True, they suggest horrors, but the horrors impress me as being just a trifle theatrical. This is, to be sure, a matter of taste, perhaps also a matter of temperament. It is my misfortune to be insensitive to bogies, just as I also fail, obtusely, to appreciate the dire implications of a nomenclature bristling with Kinarths, Chaugnars, corpsy gargoyle-shapes, and Dagoth Wolds—weird terminology, without a doubt, but for me, somehow unconvincing. I much prefer Mr. Long's darkly allusive prose, wherein phantasy is enriched with a delicate imagination and shudders emerge from the incommunicable. For it is my opinion that the essence of fright evaporates as soon as it is catalogued, and that the hiding place of horror must be divined rather than revealed in the tenebrous caverns of the Unknown. Suggestion, adumbration, atmosphere, a certain *strangeness* that eludes analysis—these are the most potent ingredients of the *frisson*; Poe had the formula, also Arthur Machen and Lord Dunsany. It is a moving force in Mr. Long's prose, but not often in his verse.

While in this confessional mood, let us, as Huneker says, promenade our prejudices. I do not care very much for the poetry of mere statement; "I did this, I saw that"; no resultant inference or conclusion. The form of sonnet I like best is that in which a theme is developed in the octave, and its application resolved in the sestet. Thus the sonnet becomes contrapuntal and explicit. Such requirements may be, for all I know, extraneous to the laws of sonnet construction, but my ingenuous preference remains unshaken. Prejudices are the most unmanageable things, so I find myself unable to praise Mr. Long's "In Mayan Splendor"[7] without some reservation, mainly because it does not seem to say anything significant. He relates that he has dwelt in fabled cities, traced dark figures on the sands of alien keys, lingered in Copan and clothed himself in legendary grace; admitting the dream, you say to yourself, "so he *had*—but what of it?" The lines are musical, the imagery gorgeous, but they don't *arrive*. Surely, you feel, here is something of deep import that the poet should cogitate; the Mayan experiences of the octave should be subjected to some sort of poetic exegesis in the sestet, failing which the sonnet stands merely as an ornamental statement. To the pertinent objection that a great deal of beautiful poetry had thus been written, I can only reply that to me it is not satisfying, however objectively beautiful it may be. In short,

"I do not like thee, Doctor Fell,
The reason why I cannot tell."

Some of Mr. Long's mannerisms are also to be deplored, though in a less skillful craftsman I would pass them without comment. Such inept and feeble reiterations as

"The Goblin Tower *stood* and *stood*
And *stood* for *years* and *years*"—

and again in the same poem,

"And yet for *years* and *years*, and *years*"—

suggest the sing-song mechanics of kindergarten verse. To do Mr. Long justice the jingle may actually have been written for children. In another poem of striking but uneven quality, entitled "The White People,"[8] the houses of this curious race are described as being located

"Deep in the woods *that are not yet*"

and their equally curious "worm-dogs"

"Fly with tales *that are not told*,"

which might cause a more ribald reviewer to assume that the worm-dogs are not to be told by their tales. I like even better the sardonic lines entitled "Advice,"[9] with its grisly last line, but from "The Abominable Snow Men"[10] and other similar abominations, good Lord deliver us! I do not pretend to know the niceties of "weird" technique, and so, as Mr. Lovecraft had intimated more than once, I am hardly competent to criticize them; but surely there must be some boundaries beyond which it is unsafe to venture—some excesses of the grotesque and the unintelligible which are apt to react upon the ordinary reader in the fatal form of amusement, rather than horror. The point is at least debatable, though I can easily imagine several crushing retorts, one of which might be, "If you are so sensitive and literal-minded as to misunderstand weird stories, why read them?" In another mood, "Great Ashtoreth"[11] shows the poet to better advantage, though marred by the final weak line, wherein "alway" is illicitly wedded to "away" without benefit of clergy—or prosody.

But enough of fault-finding. These trivial defects are quite evidently the result of youthful haste, and God knows I should have been hanged long ago on the same gibbet! In this same book Mr. Long's ability is shown in poems that reveal more mature powers. I wish that I might be able to sign my name to a rollicking lyric as "Pirate Men," to such a vital and gripping sonnet as "Subway," to such singing and lovely verses as "Mary Magdalene," or to such vigorous, exotic characterization as "West

Indies." The classical adaptations are light and graceful, though lacking a copy of the Roman epigrammatist's works here in my bookless exile, I am a bit hazy as to whether "Apollinaris" refers to the well-known mineral water, or to the Bishop of Laodicea (both a trifle anachronistic) or some figure in Martial[12] or in myth that for the moment eludes my memory. At any rate, Apollinaris manages to catch "a fish elate," which is something. The exquisite lines beginning

"Sermio's greenness falls—"

are as beautiful and as evasive as anything written by Jules La Forgue or Arthur Symons, and the sonnet[13] on page 17 is a noble and impressive revelation of the poet's genuine talent.

Mr. Long, I am told, has passed from idle amateur[14] dalliance to the more rewarding uplands of professional writing; he can therefore well afford to smile indulgently at these unimportant opinions, reflecting that the cheques he receives from his publishers are an irrefutable retort to all carping critics.

Editor's Notes

[1]Robert H. Barlow.

[2]Frank Belknap Long. *The Goblin Tower*. Cassia, Florida: The Dragon Fly Press, c. Fall 1935.

[3]"When Chaugnar Wakes," *Weird Tales* 20, No. 2 (Sept 1932): 410. Great Chaugnar Faugn is Long's elephantine entity from the short novel "The Horror from the Hills."

[4]"On Icy Kinarth," *Weird Tales* 15, No. 4 (Apr. 1930): 444.

[5]*Weird Tales* 15, No. 2 (Feb. 1930): 267.

[6]"An Old Wife Speaketh It," *The United Amateur* 25, No. 2 (May 1926): 2.

[7]*Weird Tales* 23, No. 4 (Apr. 1934): 519.

[8]*Weird Tales* 10, No. 5 (Nov. 1927): 633.

[9]*Weird Tales* 9, No. 5 (June 1927): 831.

[10]*Weird Tales* 17, No. 4 (June/July 1931): 559.

[11]*Weird Tales* 16, No. 5 (Nov. 1930): 673.

[12]Here Edkins is referring to "Martial: The Vacationist."

[13]"Sonnet," which won FBL the Edna St. Vincent Millay Award in *Pulpsmith* Magazine in Summer 1984.
[14]Oddly enough, Edkins remarks that Long has passed from amateur journalism into professional writing—many of the poems in *The Goblin Tower* appeared professionally in *Weird Tales*.

From "With the Editor" by George Steele Seymour

IN *THE STEP LADDER* (OCT. 1926)

A Man from Genoa and Other Poems by Frank Belknap Long Jr., is published by W. Paul Cook of Athol, Mass. The author is a young man of New York and he has not yet found his key, but the book shows a bent towards romanticism that may grow into something of greater proportions. He should not let his imagination run into ungainly expression but should spend more effort in trying to find the inevitable word. Slender as it is, this book contains much that should not have been published, yet there are unmistakable signs that the author, if he works hard enough, will someday do better.

From "The World of Books" by Isaac Goldberg

IN *HALDEMAN-JULIUS WEEKLY* (APRIL 24, 1926)

***A Man from Genoa and Other Poems.* By Frank Belknap Long, Jr. With a Preface by Samuel Loveman. Athol, Mass. The Recluse Press.**

***Each in His Time.* By Nathan Rosenbaum. Ariel Publishing Company. Philadelphia.**

There has been a complaint, and a legitimate one, I believe, that the American drama has been tending toward the deceiving depths of intellectualism. That art should exist without intellect is a most unintelligent expectation; the artist is no mere emotional jellyfish, minus backbone. Neither is he, on the other hand, an intellectual rhinoceros, all insentient hide. He feels with his brain as well as with his heart; he writes, too, with both. Let him hearken to his heart alone and he produces some formless monster of the intuitions, which are wonderful slaves but terrible masters; let him hearken to his brain alone and he produces a monster of form like those nuts that are all shell and nothing within. What has been true of American drama is true of its poetry. To alter but slightly an excellent witticism of Brander Matthews, our younger writers have swayed between the phallic and the cephalic; either their excessive emotionalism has led them too directly to sex or their equally excessive intellectualism has induced a desiccation of the feelings.

Mr. Rosenbaum, in general, has not yet achieved the firm form required by his none too original themes. He has felt what we all feel in our progress through adolescence to adulthood—has felt it with more poignancy in the experience than skill at imparting it. Now and then a fine line flashes across the page, only to be ruined in effect by a clumsy inversion, a pedestrian expression, a limping cadence. He is riper emotionally than technically; he has not yet achieved the necessary fusion of both. Mr. Long, technically much more proficient, is emotionally more restrained, and as a result, one comes the easier to believe him. His lines, utterly apart from their subject matter, carry poetic conviction. His themes are not trite, if more than one is conventional. He makes no attempts at an outward formal freedom, yet moves freely within the forms he has chosen.

I select a short piece to suggest Mr. Long's promise; is a simple thing called "A Time Will Come":

A time will come when we shall share
The wonder, dear, together,
Of flaming candles on a shrine
In gray and golden weather.
And we shall kneel with avid eyes
To watch a shining chalice
By children borne across the nave
Of some cathedral-palace.
And we shall rise, and go away
With eager lips that cling,
Unmindful of the strumming choirs
And every living thing.

LIFE AND ART—ONE ASPECT

To make of life an art is one thing; to make of art a life is another. He who lives for art alone has not made of life an art. The essence of art is in rare thrills that must not be too frequently repeated. The art of life, on the other hand, is to husband the experience out of which those thrills in their due season burst forth. To hear too much music, to gaze too long at too many pictures, to read too much in the same field, is to practice a subtle form of self-drugging. We must go back often to the cruder life whence art derives its quintessential vitality. Those who "live only for art" have made of it an escape from life, which is to true living, what opium-visions are to the glories of fields and waters. The artistry of living knows that thrills, from their very nature, must be relatively rare.

A brief letter to FBL from Edwin Arlington Robinson

99 St. Botolph Street
Boston, April 13, 1926

Dear Mr. Long,

Many thanks for your book, which suggests strongly something more important to come. Please don't be in too great a hurry.

Yours Sincerely,
E.A. Robinson

[Edwin Arlington Robinson - 13 April 1926]

Poet Edwin Arlington Robinson (1869 – 1935)

IN MAYAN SPLENDOR Reviewed by Donald Sidney-Fryer

FROM *NYCTALOPS* 14 (MARCH 1978)

This book is purely unalloyed gold together with some silver of similar quality. For once, amid the busy production of fantastic verse, we have here at last the real McCoy, verily the genuine article. What a relief! what a pleasure! what a joy! Along with the work of George Sterling, Clark Ashton Smith, Samuel Loveman and others, this must rank with the more notable imaginative poetry of the twentieth century. Belknap Long's fine craftsmanship permits us to enjoy, unsullied and unflawed, his poetic visions, narratives and outpourings. The volume is physically slender but the contents themselves are ponderous in quality. Endless notable and endlessly quotable, these poems cover a wide spectrum of mood and emotion: from the opening sonnet In Mayan Splendor ("In misty dreams and shadowed memories / Of fabled cities I have dwelt apace.") to the final selection, the touching memories sonnet H.P. Lovecraft ("Sublimer beauty never dwelt with Poe, / Or walked with Shelley in the white dawn's glow.") our poet ranges far afield indeed. We have here such wonderfully imaginative and narrative lyrics as *A Knight of La Mancha, A Man from Genoa, The Magi, The Ballad of St. Anthony, An Old Tale Retold, The Goblin Tower, The Marriage of Sir John de Mandeville, The Horror on Dagoth Wold, Ballad of Mary Magdalene,*

Great Ashtoreth, and An Old Wife Speaketh It. To quote from *When We Have Seen:*

Let us mount gorgeous horses
For sea-grit cities beckon
And we go Troyward soon.
Yes, but let them be *Stallions of the Moon!*
Mystic beasts of Sibyl,
Fed on golden oats,
More than Spartan finish
On their moonspun coats.

Belknap Long's own poem titled *The Hashish Eater* is quite different from Clark Ashton Smith's towering magnum opus of the same name but it is nonetheless appealing and certainly surprising in its own way:

The boat was waiting; seas like foaming wine
Curled round its prow; the moon was full and red.
"I go," he laughed, "to lie upon her bed
And kiss her mouth, until desire is dead,
For I am Caesar, and the world is mine!"
He shrieked, and woke upon a cross; his bands
Were dripping blood upon the yellow sands,
And far below a harlot wrung her hands.

Our own first introduction to Belknap Long's fanciful and sensitive muse came via H.P. Lovecraft's monumental essay "Supernatural Horror in Literature" in the latter's discussion of the Anglo-Welsh fantaisiste Arthur Machen and his works. Within his discussion HPL quotes in full the superb sonnet *On Reading Arthur Machen*; by virtue of which we became an instantaneous but permanent fan of Belknap Long's. We in our turn cannot resist quoting this poem in full yet once again:

There is a glory in the autumn wood,
The ancient lanes of England wind and climb
Past wizard oaks and gorse and tangled thyme
To where a fort of mighty empire stood:
There is a glamour in the autumn sky;
The reddened clouds are writhing in the glow

Of some great fire, and there are glints below
Of tawny yellow where the embers die
I wait, for he will show me, clear and cold,
High-raised in splendor, sharp against the North
The Roman eagles, and through mists of gold
The marching legions as they issue forth:
I wait, for I would share with him again
The ancient wisdom, and the ancient pain.

Shades of the (British) Masterpiece Theatre production of *I, Claudius,* that emperor under whose rule Britain was added to the *Imperium Romanium!* Could there be any better allusion to, and summary of, the unique feeling and attraction characteristic of Machen's *oeuvre* than this? We doubt it.

Or in another and more contemporary mood Belknap Long can charm us with such a simple, tranquil, delightful lyric as *A Time Will Come:*

A time will come when we shall share
The wonder, dear, together,
Of flaming candles on a shrine
In gray and golden weather.
And we shall kneel with avid eyes,
To watch a shining chalice
By children borne across the nave
Of some cathedral-palace.
And we shall rise, and go away
With eager lips that cling,
Unmindful of the strumming choirs
And every living thing.

It seems incredible to us that Belknap Long could have created *Exotic Quest* at the age of eighteen! But as fine as are these more fanciful effusions, in such pieces as *In Hospital, Manhattan Skyline, W.W., and Subway,* our poet effects his own unique and literally neat amalgam of classic form with contemporary allusion and subject-matter, the past and present nicely intermingling for present as well as future delectation.

Withal, his characteristic touch and treatment are light, but not slight; we might even say lightsome in the best sense of something nimble, buoyant, lively, graceful, cheerful, and lighthearted but also in the sense of something literally luminous and bright.

Since much imaginative poetry of the past and present has had a distinct and distinctive tendency toward the massively, but not necessarily unattractively, ponderous in effect, Belknap Long's achievement in his own verse must be seen as all the more remarkable.

We understand that the contents of this volume, collecting as it does his early poetry, has been subjected to some judicious and recent revision, thus making *In Mayan Splendor* in some sense as much a product of the mature Belknap Long as of the earlier poet before the age of thirty. While there is frankly far less cosmic-mindedness, or cosmic-astronomic-mindedness, such as we associate with HPL or Ashton Smith, there is instead a far-ranging fancy which, in the final analysis, has its own incidental touches and elements of cosmicism. Together with the chiseled and incisive prose of Samuel Loveman's *Preface*, and with the simply gorgeous illustrations by Stephen Fabian—my wouldn't the designs for *Stallions of the Moon* and *The Goblin Tower* make equally gorgeous posters?!—*In Mayan Splendor*, truly a cyclic recapitulation of Belknap Long's lyrical youth, forms a perfect little book, truly a delightful gift for yourself or for some fortunate friend. It ranks as one of the handsomest books Arkham House has yet produced under the aegis of the current managing editor James Turner. *By all means!*

FBL circa 1920

FBL circa 1981

About the Author

By Perry M. Grayson

FRANK BELKNAP LONG, JR. (April 27, 1901 – January 3, 1994) is the prolific World Fantasy Award winning author of such books as *The Hounds of Tindalos, The Horror from the Hills* and *The Rim of the Unknown.* Incidentally, those titles are three of the most sought-after collector's items published by Arkham House, the specialty press founded in 1939 by August Derleth and Donald Wandrei to immortalize the writings of H. P. Lovecraft.

Lovecraft discovered Long and took him under his wing after reading FBL's story "The Eye Above the Mantel" in *The United Amateur* in 1921. The two became best friends during the early 1920s while Lovecraft lived in New York. They exchanged hundreds of letters over the course of 15 years. The Lovecraft association tends to keep "Belknapius" (as he was called by HPL) in HPL's shadow, but Long's body of work speaks for itself.

Fiction-wise, FBL primarily wrote in the realms of science fiction, fantasy, horror, adventure and mystery. Over the course of his seven-decade career Long wrote over 300 stories, poems and articles, many of which have been widely reprinted in over 80 major publisher anthologies. Long's first professionally published story was "The Desert Lich," which appeared in the November 1924 issue of *Weird Tales.* His first book was *A Man from Genoa and Other Poems* (1926). The Long legacy is an important one in the annals of 20th century pop culture. He helped shape the fantasy, horror and science fiction fields while Ray Bradbury and Isaac Asimov were still in their teens. Long was one of the few early science fiction writers to make the transition from the 1930s *Astounding Stories* to exacting editor John W. Campbell's *Astounding Science Fiction* and *Unknown* during SF's Golden Age. In the pages of *Astounding* and

Unknown, Long appeared alongside Asimov, Robert Heinlein, Theodore Sturgeon, A.E. van Vogt, Fritz Leiber, Henry Kuttner, C.L. Moore, Eric Frank Russell and many other highly respected SF luminaries. When the pulp magazines died in the mid-1950s, Long successfully made the transition to the paperback original. As a pioneering horror comic book script writer, Long paved the way for the immensely popular EC comics with his work in the ACG title *Adventures into the Unknown* (circa 1948). As an editor, Frank worked on magazines such as *Fantastic Universe*, *Satellite Science Fiction*, *Short Stories* and *Mike Shayne Mystery* during the 1950s and 1960s. Long's poetic bent carried over into his prose, and his verse kept the torch of romantic tradition alight during the age of modern free form poetry.

FBL was honored with the Lifetime Achievement award from the World Fantasy Convention in 1978 and the Bram Stoker award for Lifetime Achievement from the Horror Writers of America in 1987. You might think that an author with such laurels would have enjoyed the success of modern horror acolytes like Stephen King, Dean Koontz and Anne Rice, but Frank Long's existence was that of the struggling artist. Not a surprise when you consider Edgar Allan Poe's demise. An empty bank account, but a *wealth* of imagination.

Long outlived most of his fellow pulp-era writers, and he made a final public appearance at the Lovecraft Centennial Conference in Providence, RI, in 1990. A New Yorker at heart, Long spent most of his life in the Big Apple—aside from a brief stint in California during World War II. He married Lyda Arco in 1961. Frank and Lyda had no children. Lyda was very protective of her husband's literary reputation, always reminding folks that Frank was much more than just Lovecraft's protégé. Long passed away on January 2, 1994. His spirit lives on in every word he wrote.

About the Editor

PERRY M. GRAYSON was born in Chicago, Illinois, on March 11, 1975. Perry's family relocated to Southern California during his early years. He lived in the San Fernando Valley, capital of the pornography industry and the setting of the film *Fast Times at Ridgemont High*, until 2006. Perry now resides in Sydney, Australia, with his wife Tanya, an entertainment industry veteran, and two cats.

Perry founded Tsathoggua Press in 1994 to publish pulp-era fantasy, horror and mystery fiction and non-fiction works relating to vintage authors. Since 1995, Perry has edited four volumes by his favorite author, Frank Belknap Long: *Escape from Tomorrow* (Necronomicon Press), *The Eye Above the Mantel*, *The Darkling Tide* (Tsathoggua Press) and the present collection. Many more FBL projects are in the works.

Perry's pro writing career began in 1994 as a journalist for electronic news service SilentRadio. Between 1997 and 2007 Perry served as copywriter and production coordinator for Sampson Advertising West, a busy porn graphic design and advertising agency.

Perry's other passion is music, and his pro music career took flight between 1997 and 2000 as guitarist and main songwriter in the heavy metal band Destiny's End. With Destiny's End, he recorded two albums on Metal Blade Records and embarked on a regional tour of Texas with labelmates Mercyful Fate in 1998. A full US tour with metal mavens Nevermore and Iced Earth followed in 1999. The US tour was followed by an appearance in front of tens of thousands of screaming metalheads at the illustrious Wacken Open Air Festival in Germany in August 1999—alongside a European tour with Sacred Steel, Wardog and Slough Feg.

Next, Perry formed technical/progressive metal band Artisan, tackling both aggressive vocals and guitar from 2000-2003. While in Artisan, Perry supported internationally renowned metal artists such as Arch Enemy, Strapping Young Lad, Cathedral, Samael, Engine, Hate Eternal, Nile, Zero Hour, Onward and others.

Since 2002, Perry has fronted the loud, raw vintage heavy rock power trio Falcon as guitarist/vocalist with friend and collaborator Greg Lindstrom, co-founder of cult U.S. metal legends Cirith Ungol. Towards the end of Perry's tenure in Artisan (and simultaneous to Falcon) he played guitar for multinational metal project Isen Torr on the EP *Mighty and Superior* (2003). Branching out further, he played bass for American heavy doom rockers Pale Divine on a European tour in 2005 with Place of Skulls (led by Pentagram guitarist Victor Griffin).

Aside from music, Perry's pop-culture expertise extends far beyond to vintage TV, film and literature. He was a staff writer for *Metal Maniacs*, one of the *world's* largest circulation heavy metal magazines, for over a decade.

Since the mid-1990s, Perry has contributed fiction, non-fiction, interviews, reviews and poetry to such mags and sites as *The Scream Factory, Crypt of Cthulhu, Necrofile, Other Dimensions, Snakepit, Fungi, Al Azif, Emptywords.org, Slow Ride, Hellridemusic.com, Snap Pop!, Hot Metal* and a host of others. He is often asked by hard rock and metal bands to pen liner notes and bios.

A true-crime buff and lifelong devotee of American hardboiled literature, Perry often ventures out of the armchair, prowling deep into unsolved cold cases with abandon. His latest true-crime project, tentatively titled *Dirty Deeds in L.A.*, focuses on weird crimes of the 1940s, including the Black Dahlia Murder case.

Perry Grayson on stage in Hollywood with Falcon

Books by Frank Belknap Long

A Man from Genoa and Other Poems
The Goblin Tower
The Hounds of Tindalos
John Carstairs, Space Detective
Space Station No. 1
Woman from Another Planet
The Mating Center
The Horror Expert
Mars Is My Destination
The Horror from the Hills
Three Steps Spaceward
It Was the Day of the Robot
The Martian Visitors
Mission to a Star
Odd Science Fiction
So Dark a Heritage
This Strange Tomorrow
Lest Earth Be Conquered.
Journey Into Darkness
...And Others Shall Be Born
The Three Faces of Time
To The Dark Tower (as by Lyda Belknap Long)
Monster from Out of Time
Survival World
The Witch Tree (as by Lyda Belknap Long).
The Shape of Fear (as by Lyda Belknap Long)
The Night of the Wolf
The Rim of the Unknown.

House of the Deadly Nightshade (as by Lyda Belknap Long)
Legacy of Evil (as by Lyda Belknap Long)
Crucible of Evil (as by Lyda Belknap Long)
The Early Long
Howard Phillips Lovecraft: Dreamer on the Nightside
In Mayan Splendor
The Lemoyne Heritage (as by Lyda Belknap Long)
Night Fear
Autobiographical Memoir
Escape from Tomorrow
The Eye Above the Mantel and Other Stories
The Darkling Tide

www.ingramcontent.com/pod-product-compliance
Lightning Source LLC
Chambersburg PA
CBHW070820020826
48982CB00014B/140
9781763524507